"A must-read for every woman who wants to know how to create more success and satisfaction in her life."

—Jack Canfield, Co-author, *Chicken Soup for the Woman's Soul* ®

"What you are about to experience is a journey of excellence hosted by women of wisdom. Their inspiration will lead you to know what you want, believe you deserve it, and be willing to do whatever it takes to get it."

—Gail Cohen, Professional Speaker and Author of *Personal Best* and *Thinking Outside the Lines*

"Ordinary Women, Extraordinary Success *will, without exception, give you the secrets, techniques, and information that will enable you to learn what it takes to tap into the inner strength we all have to reach self-actualization."*

—Carol E. Scott, Chairman, TOURVEST, South Africa

"This sensible book is a no-nonsense guide for women and girls. It not only encourages women to improve societal and workplace conditions, the information contained within will enable women to achieve their full potential."

—Lois Sagel, International Programme Director, Soroptimist International, "A Global Voice for Women"

"This book is fabulous. The impact it will have on women will be phenomenal because it offers concrete methods to resolve the dilemmas we all face every day."

—Julie Neil, General Manager, UPN Las Vegas— KTUD-TV, and Founding President, Women in Communications

ORDINARY WOMEN...
EXTRAORDINARY SUCCESS

Everything You Need to Excel, From America's Top Women Motivators

Dr. Courtney Anderson

Tara Bazar

Jane Boucher

Fiona Carmichael

Dr. Chérie Carter-Scott

JoAnn Corley

Jennifer Buck Curtet

Jan Elliott

Jan Fraser

Claudia James

Leanne Mackenzie

Debbie Metzger

Judi Moreo

Pam Royle

Sharon Spano

Jana Stanfield

Lisa Walker

Jill Wesley

Candy Whirley

CAREER PRESS

Franklin Lakes, NJ

ORDINARY WOMEN...EXTRAORDINARY SUCCESS
TYPESET BY STACEY A. FARKAS
Cover design by Lu Rossman/Digi Dog Design
Printed in the U.S.A. by Book-mart Press

"Are You a Negaholic" quiz © 1987 Dr. Chérie Carter-Scott.
"The Dash" © Alton Maiden.
"If I Were Brave" by Jana Stanfield and Jimmy Scott, copyright Jana Stan Tunes/English Channel Music (ASCAP)

To order this title, please call toll-free 1-800-CAREER-1 (NJ and Canada: 201-848-0310) to order using VISA or MasterCard, or for further information on books from Career Press.

The Career Press, Inc., 3 Tice Road, PO Box 687,
Franklin Lakes, NJ 07417
www.careerpress.com

Library of Congress Cataloging-in-Publication Data available upon request.
ISBN 1-56414-701-0

Dedication

We dedicate this book to the Extraordinary Women in our lives—our mothers, grandmothers, and friends. We celebrate who they are and who they were. We thank them for all they sacrificed for us and for their unceasing encouragement and love. Their words live on in our hearts and minds.

Dr. Courtney Anderson
Kathleen Whitlock Anderson

Tara Bazar
Cookie Panno-Penton

Jane Boucher
Virginia Lee

Fiona Carmichael
Diana Carmichael

Dr. Chérie Carter-Scott
Dr. Earle F. Pomije

JoAnn Corley
Marguerite Robinson

Jennifer Buck Curtet
Sharyn Davis, Wendy Buck

Jan Elliott
Elvera Crowell

Jan Fraser
Sadie Beverly Woroshilsky Fraser, Jennie Woroshilsky

Claudia James
Edna Mae Henderson Hinton (Maizie)

Leanne Mackenzie
Marion L. Rose

Debbie Metzger
Annette Theriault Sanderson

Judi Moreo
Daisy Shropshire-Roberts

Pam Royle
Dorotha Mapes Gee (Dot)

Sharon Spano
Isabel Vega

Jana Stanfield
*Nancy McCasland Ferguson, Luellen Stanfield,
and Olga McCasland Dickie*

Lisa Walker
Elisa M. Laude

Jill Wesley
Helaine Wesley

Candy Whirley
Virginia Henderson

Contents

Success of the Heart, 15

Success of the Mind, 79

Success of the Soul, 167

Preface

BY JAN FRASER

It took *Time, Idea, Purpose,* and *Opportunity* converging at the same moment for the dream of this book to become a reality.

The *Time* is now, though it's been years in the making.

The *Idea* is essential—supporting, nurturing, and "knowledge-sharing" for women.

The *Purpose* is to provide you—and women everywhere—moments of motivational magic and the practical tips and advice to accomplish anything you want in life.

The *Opportunity* is this book, which you hold in your hands because of our far-thinking, supportive publisher, Ron Fry, and my mentor BG, who gave me the idea for this book in the first place!

It sometimes takes *Time* for seeds planted in love and self-esteem to nurture and grow. My mother, Sadie, who overcame countless obstacles to become a registered nurse in 1931, made the prediction that I would write a book and speak to people everywhere someday. Unbelievable! What she saw in me, *I* surely didn't. I used to hide under the wicker planter stand when I wanted to be invisible. Her thoughts about my future and what I could do were outrageous. And yet, they took root inside me, down in that deep, safe place where dreams are kept.

Knowing Mom had the confidence in me to write and co-author a book created my focus and my goal. At times, when I doubted myself, I'd remember something she told me before she passed away in 1991: "We carry our mentors with us wherever we go and whatever we do." And sometimes it takes *Time* for the words to convince us we really *can* do it!

The *Idea* for the book is a creative endeavor that grew in intensity over the years as I experienced life and absorbed new information. Let's live our lives like a marathon, not a sprint to that finish line. Let's not be in such a hurry to get there. Let's enjoy and celebrate our Extraordinary Success throughout our journey.

The *Purpose* for the book was given to me by *you*. I've spoken to you and your friends, cousins, and coworkers all over the world. I've heard your needs and your concerns for keeping it all together, tackling the ruts in the road, and recognizing who you are and what you are accomplishing. I wanted all of us to have access to a book *for* women, *by* women.

To accomplish this purpose, not just any women authors would do. I wanted top professionals who have been out there, like myself, speaking and inspiring women for decades. I can assure you—the 18 other women in this book *are* the best! And an amazingly varied group—ranging in age from their 20s to their 60s (and beyond); raised on farms, in cities; U.S.-born and foreign-born; with diverse cultural, economic, and spiritual backgrounds. I am thrilled and honored to call them friends and colleagues.

Opportunity occurred in January, 2003, when I met Ron Fry and asked him to help me publish a life-changing book for women. I wanted a volume filled with teaching points and real-life stories. A book to tuck under our pillows at night. A book we wouldn't dare let out of our sight or lend to a friend. I wanted a book to celebrate the Extraordinary Success of Women and detail how we can *all* get more from our lives by listening to women who have been where we've been and are going where we want to go.

So here it is—a warming gift for you, your friends, your mothers, and your sisters. We celebrate *your* Extraordinary Success.

Women alone are unsinkable. Women united are unstoppable. Feel the strength, support and love in these pages. Perhaps this is *your Time*—with an *Idea* and *Purpose*—to grab the *Opportunity* that's waiting for you!

Good Luck and *bon voyage!*

Jan Fraser
September, 2003

Jan Fraser

HOW DO *YOU* DEFINE SUCCESS?

What is success? (Let's leave *extraordinary* success aside for a minute!)

Is it something general and a little hazy: *joy, happiness, satisfaction?*

Or practical and defined—a stable marriage or relationship, enough money, nurturing your children, a satisfying job or career?

Do we have to wait a lifetime to recognize it, as if we were checking off a 75-year-old "to-do" list?

Or do we find ourselves measuring it day-by-day, toting up the victories and defeats of our more-than-hectic lives? In other words, is success perhaps just surviving?

I'm sure if I asked 100 women to define "success," I'd get a hundred different responses. And certainly when I asked 18 other authors to write about the key ingredients of *extraordinary* success, they had rather different ideas, from the ephemeral "attitude" and "passion" to the more practical—honoring our mothers and raising our daughters.

They are all valid definitions. They are all valid ingredients. To *someone*...maybe you. So I will now add my very own definitions of success and extraordinary success. Success is getting out of bed in the morning and moving steadily toward your desired goal—a degree, a new skill, a new job, a new love, surviving a major illness or the loss of a loved one. Extraordinary success is being able to do it *every single day*.

And although there are already quite a few examples in this book to illustrate extraordinary success—the authors as well as the stories they tell—I must add two more here.

Rhonda Anderson

Rhonda Anderson grew up in a home that treasured the simple act of putting photos into albums as a wonderful way to capture family memories and savor them for future enjoyment. It was a tradition started by her mother, and one that would lead Rhonda down a path she could little expect when she was just a youngster.

In 1987, her sister asked if Rhonda, the family's "picture historian," could teach a 35-minute class on how to properly save and store photos. Rhonda was deluged with questions and orders for the albums she spoke about—the ones she used herself. She got excited—she had clearly identified a need. Now she just needed a way to fill it.

Unfortunately, she had just received a postcard from Webway, the manufacturer, informing her that the particular album she (and her mother) used had been discontinued. With orders for 40 albums in hand, she called the company after hours to see what she could do. Serendipitously, the new vice-president of sales, Cheryl Lightle, was working late and took the call.

Webway had always concentrated on selling through retail outlets. When Cheryl heard that Rhonda had sold 40 albums during a single class, she was intrigued and invited her to travel to the company's Minnesota headquarters to show them in person how she managed to sell albums like Tupperware. (She also let Rhonda know that the album she had been using had *not* been discontinued.)

Meanwhile, Rhonda learned that a local home and garden show was scheduled, and 15,000 people were supposed to attend. Although she was confident she could sell an album to every attendee, to be conservative, she ordered "only" 1,000. She and her husband had recently sold their home. Rhonda took virtually all the equity to buy a van, a computer, and the 1,000 albums.

She sold 60 and had to pack the remaining 940 into her garage. But she had generated 500 leads. She called each one of them back...and scheduled five home classes a week for five months. The albums were soon gone.

While she was proving that people were hungry for the "Creative Memories" she offered, Cheryl had been working back at headquarters.

In July, 1987, the manufacturer made Rhonda an offer—keep doing what she was doing, but as a consultant to their new direct sales division, which they would name Creative Memories (*www.creativememories.com*). By the end of the year, she had added five other consultants to her team. Today there are almost 80,000 consultants in eight countries, and Webway's sales will top half a billion dollars this year.

When I asked Rhonda to share her "secrets" of extraordinary success, she said two things that might seem weird or eccentric, but that she claimed were the keys to her own success:

1. Deviate from the usual.
2. Deviate from the acceptable.

In 1988, Rhonda loaded up a 30-foot trailer with albums; her husband, Mac; her four children aged 2,4,6, and 8, and traveled around the country to promote the Creative Memories mission. Usual or acceptable? Hardly.

What will *you* do in the next day, week, month, or year that is not usual or acceptable to meet *your* goals?

Ilene Ellsworth

Another extraordinarily successful woman is Ilene Ellsworth, the first director for Jafra Cosmetics who is still going strong after 44 years in the business. She told me she loved discovering just how powerful a girl born in a log cabin in rural Wyoming could be. She loved turning to women she cared about and saying, "Come on, if I can do it, you can, too!" and then watching them do it!

Her first commission check in 1960 was for $95, and she was thrilled! She certainly never dreamed then that her sales would generate a six-figure annual income for the past 20 years.

When she started selling cosmetics, she told me, she faithfully followed what her managers told her to do. But their techniques didn't seem to work for her. No matter how hard she tried, her sales were flat.

One morning she woke up, looked in the mirror and decided to put *herself* into her sales presentations, not try to parrot someone else's techniques. Within weeks, her sales topped the charts. What did she learn, and what is the lesson she hopes this book imparts to you? Absorb whatever you need to from others, but create your own style. There is only one Extraordinary You!

Whose Life Are You Living?

A woman made her way to the front of the room at the end of a Women's Conference I had led. She said I had made a difference in her life that day, and she had a message that might make a difference for me.

Her sister was dying, she told me, and there was nothing that could be done for her. But she had already taught her a wonderful lesson, one she wanted to share with me. Her sister had said to her, "When you get to the end of your life, make sure it is *your* life you've been living and not someone else's."

How many of us are living the life someone else wants us to? How many of us are *doing* things because someone else wants us to, not because *we* want to?

Perhaps that young woman's sister gave us the best definition of extraordinary success: Living our own lives...and loving them.

We may sometimes *think* we are ordinary women. The reality is, we are *all* extraordinary.

Do you have an inspiring story to share? A question? A comment? A rave?

We want to hear from you. Please send all of the above to jan@womensconferences.org.

And if you think any of our fabulous authors would be an ideal keynoter, speaker, or trainer for your company or group, please contact them directly (see their bios at the end of each chapter) or through womensconferences.org.

Thank you for your help and support!

Success
of the
Heart

Fiona Carmichael

BUILDING A BETTER TOMORROW

L ife is not always easy. There's no question that some people just seem to have it easier than others. But everyone at some point will have an obstacle in life they will have to overcome. I've yet to meet someone who hasn't.

It's been my observation that people deal with obstacles in one of two ways. Some people choose to focus on solutions, not allowing anything to get in the way of achieving their goals. Then there are those people who take virtually no responsibility for solving their problems themselves. Which are you?

Overcoming obstacles actually serves two purposes: to heighten your belief in yourself and to strengthen your determination to succeed. For many people, obstacles cause them to find a more positive meaning in life.

There are other people, of course, who use obstacles as an excuse for not being successful. After all, what could they do? They wanted to succeed, but circumstances prevented them! Don't let that person be you. It is an intelligent person who sees obstacles as something to be overcome. This viewpoint brings them closer to getting what they want. Be *this* person!

Obstacles and hardships don't have to lead to failure. Look at them in a different light. When the army of Israel faced the giant, Goliath, they said, "He's so big, we can't beat him." But when young

David saw Goliath, he said, "He's so big, I can't miss him!" Obstacles are opportunities in disguise that, when handled without fear, can transform our lives.

Obstacles Take Root

My story begins on November 11, 1965 when Ian Smith, the Prime Minister of Rhodesia, unilaterally declared independence by formally cutting ties with Britain. It was a fateful decision. From that day on, Rhodesia became an international outlaw. Sanctions were imposed, and the country was subjected to immense vilification from the rest of the world. The struggle for freedom changed from a constitutional and political fight to a military battle.

I was a little girl then, but my memory of those dim days is still with me. This major event was to dramatically affect each and every person I knew for many years to come.

I didn't know what the reasons were for declaring independence. I didn't even understand what a declaration of independence meant. Nor, quite honestly, did I care. In my innocence, nothing seemed to be very different to me. I still went to school and played with my friends every day. Life was the same.

At least that's what I thought, until early in 1966 when a farmer and his wife, the Viljoens, were murdered. Later, a Centenary farm was machine-gunned and an 8-year-old girl was killed. From those moments on, nothing was ever the same again. We were at war.

This was a secret, silent, ugly little war totally unsupported by the world beyond—small when compared with World War II or Vietnam. Judging by events in Zimbabwe today, we were right in our fight, and the rest of the world was wrong. The intimidation, anarchy, and killing still continues, all to keep one communist president in power.

It was a hard, painstaking war to fight. No family remained untouched by violence, psychological pressures, or shortages of all commodities caused by sanctions from beyond our borders.

Necessity Is the Mother of Invention

I was married on December 23, 1972. I was a teenager. The following year, my first son was born; in 1976 my second son was born. As best we could, we attempted to live a normal life. But by 1978, after losing two members of our family and countless friends, we could stand it no longer.

We realized that no matter what, life in Rhodesia would never be the same and the insurmountable obstacles were radically impacting our lives. As difficult as it was to accept, we had to make tough decisions. We decided to take charge of our destiny.

Obstacles we faced included having very little access to our money—families were only allowed to take $200 annually. Survival was a challenge. We had to be creative in finding a way to move assets. Eventually we concluded that our main objective was to find a way to move our assets into another form. This was absolutely critical to being able to build a successful life in a new country.

Our solution was to build a 56-foot ocean-going vessel. It would be large enough to smuggle supplies for everyday living as well as various other items that could later produce revenue.

To many people, this plan was unrealistic. After all, there was one thing wrong with it—we didn't have an ocean! This didn't deter us from moving forward, though. We had options, and the resolve, determination, and belief that this was the right plan for our family. If we allowed the misgivings of others to alter our plan, it would have prevented us from building a better tomorrow.

So, in January, 1978, we began the construction of the boat, *Sabi Star* (named after the national flower of Rhodesia). We estimated that the construction would take at least three years and be done in three phases:

1. We would convert an old 18-wheeler flatbed into a 1/5 wheel. This was to be used to transport the boat to South Africa. This transformation was made more difficult by the lack of materials because of the imposed sanctions on our country.

2. We would erect the framework of the steel hull and steel plating on the newly converted 1/5 wheel. So, as the 18-wheeler was being converted, the framework for the boat was being erected simultaneously.

3. We would complete the wood work, and install equipment, machinery, and engines. It was in this phase that we would build secret storage compartments for the items to be carried out of the country.

From the moment we began the implementation of our plan, our lives were consumed by the building of the *Sabi Star*. Every spare moment was spent working on this project. It wasn't easy. There were times when we wondered if it was worth it. Knowing that we had little choice but to leave the country gave us the resolve and determination to succeed.

Six months prior to the completion of the *Sabi Star*, Prime Minister Ian Smith abdicated rule after unsuccessful negotiations with the British government. The first free election was held. Robert Mugabe, a radical communist leader, was elected to power. Overnight Rhodesia became Zimbabwe. We stepped up our work in the midst of chaos.

At last the final day came. But it was bittersweet. It was a feeling of success, but a feeling of loss as well, for we'd be leaving behind everything and everyone we'd ever known. We were stepping outside of our comfort zones.

Crossing the border from Zimbabwe into South Africa was the most frightening experience I have ever lived through. My heart pounded as the customs officials searched the boat and our vehicles for anything they deemed to be contraband. They found nothing. I looked back, and as I tucked my boys into their seats, tears rolled down my cheeks.

Expect Greatness

There are always going to be obstacles in life. The real challenge is to overcome them. When you expect great things, great things will happen. For some, an obstacle may be the "end of the line." For others with strong beliefs and great expectations, an obstacle is simply regarded as a setback. Let it be that way for you. Have faith in your future.

Sometimes overcoming obstacles also brings change. You'll be out of your comfort zone, and this can be frightening for some. Do what you're afraid to do, go where you are afraid to go, because if you allow the fear to take hold and immobilize you, opportunity may pass you by.

Attitude Is Everything

Having the right attitude will also determine how you view the things that happen to you. I've yet to see anyone overcome obstacles with a bad attitude. Choose your attitude. Imagine if I'd had the attitude that there was nothing we could do about our situation in Rhodesia. I would not be living in the United States today. Having the right attitude makes the difference in the quality of your life. It's how we view life and how we face adversity when it comes our way. Your attitude determines how you view obstacles. Attitude is everything. With a positive attitude, you can recognize obstacles as your vehicle to living a better tomorrow.

5 Steps to a Better Tomorrow

There are five powerful steps you can use to build a better tomorrow, five key tools that will enable you to overcome any obstacle. As you read, think about what actions you will need to take to really live the life you want. Your life can't change by itself. Ultimately, it's the actions you take that will make the difference between successful living and just surviving.

Step #1: Evaluation

Life is a do-it-yourself project, just like building a house. You can carefully and lovingly build a house with the right materials and it will require very little maintenance, or you can erect a sloppily built shack with inferior materials and watch it fall apart. So it is with life.

Through careful evaluation, you may discover that perhaps the path on which you have been traveling is not leading you where you'd like to go. Sit down and ask yourself: *Where am I going? Why? Where do I want to be?* Evaluating what's working, what's not working, what you want and don't want is a necessary step to achieving your goals. As you evaluate your life, determine where you're going, how you're going to get there, and what steps you need to take. You will feel an influx of power as you take control of your life.

Step #2: Determine Your Goals

What goals do you have? Are you one of those people who say, "I don't have any," or "I don't know what I want"? The longer you put off determining what you want in life, the less likely you are to live a life that is truly meaningful and purposeful. There are only so many tomorrows. The future always seems a long way off...until one day, when we wonder where all the time went.

Having goals gives you a purpose in life. They are the fuel in the furnace of achievement. Consider how much time you have left. How do you want to spend it?

Writing down your goals is a basic strategy. Yet only a small percentage of people actually commit to writing what they want for themselves. Get started! Write down what you want as well as how and when you want to achieve them. Do this at a time when you feel confident and positive. When you're panicked or when you don't feel as though you have the time, it's difficult to be open to achieving all the things you want in your life.

Step #3: Prepare for Change

Unless we prepare for change, it is unlikely that these steps will bring about the success we seek. The consequence of letting change happen without our active involvement is that we might not like where it takes us.

Instead of playing the role of spectator in your own life, take charge by participating purposely and deliberately. One of your biggest challenges will be making changes that will allow you to accomplish what is important to you. If you want to change your future, you must change what you are doing in the present. Eliminate old habits that don't produce meaningful results and do the things that will lead to a better tomorrow.

No matter what your present circumstances, you have a choice as to how you handle change. You can:

- let the change pass you by and hope for things to "return to normal."
- let the change run you over and leave you in a worse condition than you were before.
- take charge of the change and your destiny.

Proper planning and working through obstacles will enable each of us to fulfill Walt Disney's words: "If we can dream it, we can do it."

Step #4: Take Action

You have determined your plan. You know what you have to do. Now it's time to take action. You have to make things happen. In the words of Goethe:

> Are you in earnest?
> Seize this very minute;
> What you can, or dream you
> can, begin it;
> Boldness has genius, power
> and magic in it;
> Only engage and then the
> mind grows heated;
> Begin and then the work will
> be completed.

Life is what you make it. Building a better tomorrow is taking one step at a time until you've overcome your obstacles.

Step #5: Never Give Up

Anything worth doing is worth sticking with until you achieve success. Expect great things and great things will happen for you.

Years ago, Calvin Coolidge stated: "Nothing in the world can take the place of persistence. Talent will not: Nothing is more common than unsuccessful men with talent. Genius will not: Unrewarded genius is almost a proverb. Education will not: The world is full of educated derelicts. Persistence and determination alone are omnipotent. The slogan 'Press on' has solved and always will solve the problems of the human race."

By practicing these five steps, you will find yourself developing strengths, poise, and beliefs that nothing on this Earth can shake. You and I have the power to tap into our inner resources and connect with that strength that will always lead us to overcome our obstacles and allow us to build a better tomorrow.

In today's rapidly changing marketplace, Fiona knows that people are a company's greatest asset. She uses her strong business background to help people tap into their inner strengths and expand their skills. She understands the requirements for success and combines this knowledge with her ability to connect with an audience to help them achieve their goals with measurable and long-lasting results.

Using vivid descriptions and examples from her business experience and personal triumphs, Fiona helps audiences realize that every person holds the roadmap to his or her own destiny. In each of her presentations, Fiona distills her knowledge and experience in a down-to-earth and convincing style to inform, encourage, and build skills that can be implemented today for tomorrows success.

Among her clients are Cirque du Soleil, Mercedes Benz, Textron Financial Services, Johannesburg Stock Exchange, Investec Banking Group, the United States Navy, Belterra Casino Resort, Behavioral Health Services, Las Vegas Metropolitan Police, and Cathay Bank.

Fiona is the cofounder of Turning Point International, a human performance improvement company originally established in South Africa, now headquartered in Las Vegas, Nevada that has worked with hundreds of companies on three continents.

Editor's Note: As she was writing this article, Fiona learned that she had breast cancer. She assures her friends, colleagues, and readers that she is facing this obstacle with courage and hope and is even more determined to build a better tomorrow.

Jane Boucher

STAYING OUT OF ABUSIVE RELATIONSHIPS

"All changes, even the most longed for, have their melancholy; for what we leave behind us is part of ourselves; we must die to one life before we can enter into another!"

—*Anatole France*

Vicky, a 28-year-old mother of three boys, was married for nine years to a man who beat her. She stayed in the abusive relationship for the sake of her children. Although her very religious family didn't approve of the way her husband treated her, they felt it was her responsibility to keep the family together no matter what.

One night, Vicky and her children ended up at a shelter for battered women. She used her time there to get some support and explore her options. She had a high school education and no job experience. She had no source of income. She wanted to return to school and get a job, but her husband didn't want her to work. She had no daycare.

In the shelter, Vicky struggled to make the right decisions for herself and her children. But because she measured the "rightness" of her decisions by the approval she got from others, she felt she had to return to her home and family. Her parents were proud of her decision to "fulfill her responsibilities." Vicky expressed her appreciation for the safe harbor, but went home after two nights away.

The battery continued. Although her husband had a talent for leaving marks where nobody else could see them, he would also beat her about the head, claiming he was "just trying to pound some sense into her."

Vicky went to see her minister. He suggested she explore ways to make her husband happier. He explained that marriage can be stressful, and that God rewards those who forgive others. He praised her for being a good wife and a fine mother by keeping the family together.

When Vicky started having headaches, she went to see the family doctor. She told him that her husband beat her repeatedly in the head. The doctor said the headaches were stress-related.

She returned home. The headaches continued. Vicky told a friend she thought her husband was a good man and didn't mean to hurt her or the kids. But she prayed the children would stay with her parents if anything happened to her—she couldn't trust her husband, she said, to provide a safe environment. The night of that conversation, everyone thought Vicky would be okay. But Vicky evidently knew then, as she had known all along, that there was no way out for her.

On her death certificate, it said that Vicky had died of a cerebral hemorrhage.

We are living in a new world since September 11th. Terrorism is in the forefront of most of our minds. We can't get away from the memories, even if we try.

Abused women understand recurring memories.

One out of four women is abused in the United States, and she returns to her abuser eight to 11 times before she leaves for good. Each time she goes back, she's at greater risk for serious injury, even death.

Domestic violence is an epidemic in our society. It cuts across every race, gender, social and economic class. It affects 6 million families in the United States every year. It is the leading cause of injury to women between the ages of 15 and 44.

Why do women stay? Why do they return?

Most abusers act remorseful after a violent episode; most victims want to believe they will change. Because women internalize, they will often blame themselves for the violence and think that if they were only better wives or partners, it wouldn't happen.

The prospect of loneliness can be terrifying. When a woman has been married and experienced a society "made for two," it is often difficult for her to conceive of "going it alone." At some point in what has become an abusive relationship, she may have experienced emotional and physical intimacy. Now, the thought of living alone and actually taking responsibility for stepping away, even from a destructive relationship, is horrifying. It is a strong deterrent. Weighing all the possibilities and consequences, many women choose to abandon loneliness and live with abuse.

Another common reason women stay or go back is because they simply do not believe they can make it financially on their own. Dr. Lenore Walker, author of *The Battered Women,* did a study of 435 women and found that 34 percent had no access to checking accounts, 50 percent had no access to charge accounts, and 27 percent had no access to cash. So even if they flee a destructive relationship, they will often return when the money's gone. Women will often be deprived of opportunities for acquiring education and job skills—husbands will threaten to withhold support, to interfere with their jobs, or to ruin their credit ratings. In the eyes of such women, it may be worth putting up with the abuse to maintain economic security.

A sad myth claims that a bad father is better than no father at all, so an abused woman may stay or even go back because "at least he's a good father." A mother may feel her only real option is staying with the man she blames herself for picking in the first place. She rationalizes that she is keeping her family together and protecting the children. In reality, *she* may be the only safe haven for the children—she knows if she leaves her husband, he may take his anger out on them. So she decides to sacrifice herself to shield her children from her husband's wrath. However, if she concludes that she is no longer able to protect them, she will find the courage to leave. *A woman is more likely to leave to protect her children than to protect herself.*

Women who stay in violent relationships do so for a wide variety of other reasons, and the reasons she stays may well change as the violence changes forms or escalates.

First, she stays because:

- She loves him.
- She believes she can reason with him.
- She feels ashamed.
- She made a marital commitment.
- She believes he's capable of change.
- She believes she can control his rage if she just tries harder.
- She believes that if she can convince him that she loves him, his jealousy and other violent behaviors will change.

Later, she stays because:

- She loves him, but less.
- She's under pressure from family or friends to stay.
- She hopes he'll get help or change.
- She's become afraid to be alone.
- She still believes he loves and needs her.
- She doesn't know how she'll financially support herself.
- She fears for her life if she threatens to leave.

Finally, she stays because:

- He has become tremendously powerful in her eyes and she is genuinely afraid to leave.
- Her self-esteem is gone.
- He's told her (and she believes him) that no one will love her like he does.
- He threatens to kill her or the children.
- She doesn't know how to survive without him.
- She is very confused and even feels guilty.
- She is having a hard time making decisions because she is depressed and immobile.
- She no longer feels any control over her life.

- She feels hopeless and helpless.
- She's lost sight of any of her options.
- She has any number of physical symptoms/illnesses and emotional problems.
- She is suicidal.

Getting Out and Staying Out

Whether you are working with women who are hurting, trying to manage your own relationship, are leaving or have left, the seven secrets I am about to share with you will help you get out of an abusive relationship...and stay out.

Having talked to hundreds of women while doing research for my books and seminars on domestic violence, I have learned from them how to stop the revolving door of abuse. Although every survivor's story is unique, there are common threads—the seven secrets.

Destroy the Illusion

The **first secret** of staying out is to *get real and destroy the illusion*. Instead of confronting the reality of abuse, a woman will refer to her husband as "controlling" or "manipulative." The abuse may be primarily verbal and mental, which allows a woman to contend that because her husband isn't (or is only "rarely") *physically* abusive, he's not really abusive at all. Her husband (or even well-meaning family and friends) may have convinced her she "would be nothing" without him and that she couldn't make a decision or do anything by herself. So she will ride his emotional roller coaster—one day he's upset by one thing; the next day, by something else. She makes excuses for him—"He didn't mean to hurt me"; "He is just a strong man, but he'd never hurt the kids"; "I shouldn't have talked to him like that; I deserved what he did."

At some point, this woman needs to face reality: Her husband is abusing her, and it's not going to stop.

Cut Off Contact

Once you face reality and flee an abusive relationship, the **second secret** is to *cut off contact*.

Margaret left her abusive husband only to return to him three times...for the children's sake. Whenever she left, her husband would find her. He was creative in inventing ways to see her and talk with her. It would get her emotionally reconnected, and she would begin to second-guess herself and the decisions she had made. For Margaret, the third time was the charm—she left him and never returned.

Yet, on average, an abused woman returns eight to 11 times before she leaves for good...one way or another. It is vital that once you get out, you discourage communication with the abuser and do everything in your power to *stay* out.

Prepare a Financial Plan

The **third secret** for staying out is to *create a financial action plan* before you leave. Brenda knew she had to leave her abusive husband, so she began to save a little money each week and hide it in a place that only she knew about. She opened her own bank account whose statements would be mailed to a safe place. She found and made copies of her children's birth certificates, car title, insurance information and forms, social security cards, house deed, mortgage papers, marriage and drivers' licenses, bank account numbers, savings passbooks and credit cards/bank ATM cards. She also did a budget so she could determine exactly how much money she and her children needed to live. With information and plan in hand—money in the bank and a job waiting for her—Brenda fled and never looked back.

Really Put the Children First

The **fourth secret** for staying out is to *destroy the myth that "any" father is better than no father at all*. An abusive father is *not* better than no father. How are children impacted by domestic violence? Children from violent homes may exhibit numerous symptoms: They won't trust adults. They may experience anxiety attacks brought on by the fear of

violence against themselves or their mother. They may have night-
mares and/or sleep disturbances. They will learn to be people-pleasers,
and even become preoccupied with pleasing the *abusive* parent. They
may be profoundly insecure, leading to cripplingly low self-esteem.
The younger they are, the more likely they will suffer from stress-
related physical illnesses. Even if they are very bright, their school
performance will probably suffer.

Worst of all, there is a high likelihood that they will become abusers themselves.

Put Yourself First, Too

As a woman frees herself from an abusive environment, she can
take steps to enhance her self-esteem and to improve the quality of
her life. The **fifth secret** to staying out is to *learn to love yourself*. A
person with high self-esteem takes care of herself and refuses to ignore her own needs. She stops flitting from relationship to relationship looking for someone else to define who she is. She begins to
listen to her heart and trust her inner wisdom. She stops letting other
people and events determine the direction of her life. She learns what
it means to be true to herself, and does so, even if it means losing the
approval of others and risking rejection.

Seek the Help You Need

The **sixth secret** to staying out is *learning how to toughen up for the
long haul*. There are many people and organizations ready to help. With
time and support, the memories will heal.

Many national and local organizations have made a commitment
to stop the hurting and start the healing. Liz Claiborne Inc., for example, has been addressing the issue of domestic violence through its
women's work program, whose awareness and education campaign
includes billboards, TV and radio public service announcements, post-
ers, brochures, surveys, campus workshops, and mailings to "influentials"
in an effort to help end abuse.

Don't ignore abuse and terror in your home. Do something about it. Get involved. Speak out. To help or get help, call the National Domestic Violence Hotline at 1-800-799-SAFE (7233).

Heal Thyself

The **seventh secret** of staying out is learning to *focus on hope and healing.* One celebrity who has helped so many women by speaking out about her own abuse is Oprah Winfrey.

Oprah revealed some years ago that she had been in an abusive relationship. She believed that she needed a man to make her life all right. She realized she was always doing things to make him feel special. No matter how hard she tried, she could never please him. Finally, she prayed for the strength to end it. Now, of course, she revels in the truth—she was all right just as she was, and she was enough all by herself. It was only after the end of that relationship that her world began to open up for her. In the January, 2002, issue of *O: The Oprah Magazine*, she stated that the biggest mistakes in her life all stemmed from giving the power over her own life to someone else…believing that the love others had to offer was more important than the love she had to give to herself.

Healing is a lifelong process. Take the first steps.

Love yourself.

Love your kids.

Get out.

Stay out.

Jane is the founder and president of Boucher Consultants. Her clients range from small businesses to Fortune 500 companies, including GM, IBM, The United States Air Force, Merrill Lynch, the Department of Defense, and *Inc.* Magazine. A dynamic and well-known speaker, she has shared the platform with

Ross Perot, General Norman Schwarzkopf, and Dr. Bernard Siegel, among others. She holds the CSP designation from the National Speaker's Association, an honor only 8 percent of professional speakers can claim.

Before founding her business, Jane Boucher was a counselor in Sarasota, Florida. She worked with chemically dependent young people. She has her BS and MA from Ohio State University and has done doctoral work at the University of South Florida. She is currently finishing her doctorate in natural medicine. She has been an adjunct professor at the University of Dayton, Wright State University, and Sinclair Community College, in Dayton, Ohio.

Jane is the author of six books (including her latest, *How to Love the Job You Hate*). She is working on two new books: *Patients First*, to remind us that in health care the patient needs to come first, and *Surviving Him: How to Stay Out Once You Get Out*, from which this chapter was adapted.

Jane may be reached through either of her Websites, *www.janeboucher.com* or *www.janeboucher.org*.

Jennifer Buck Curtet

If You Dream It, You Can Be It

Have you ever noticed that some people appear to have been blessed with a blissful existence? They seem to dance through life, tiptoeing through the daisies and flying on clouds. They always seem to be happy and rarely have a bad day. Have you ever wondered what their secret is?

Well, I'm right there with you. I always struggled to figure out what those chipper people had that I didn't. I assumed it was an extra shot in their latte. They were never depressed, never moody, and never seemed to be stuck in a funk. Believe me, I *know* funk. I used to be that person in the office who blamed my bad attitude on everybody and everything else. If anyone gave me a funny look, I blamed my bad attitude on him or her. If the weather was lousy, I blamed my bad attitude on that. If you caught me in the morning, I would explain away my lousy mood by claiming, "I'm just not a morning person." But honestly, if you caught up with me in the afternoon, I wasn't much better!

I remember reading once that the attitude I chose every day would directly impact the results that I would enjoy in life. Of course, in my funk, I thought it was a load of bunk! I couldn't imagine that I had that much control over anything, let alone my life. But somehow, eventually, that information sunk in and started to scratch at the back of my mind. I started to think about the attitude I chose every day and what I was forced to live with at the end of each day. I looked at my internal conversations, my outlook on life, and my daily routine. I watched my reactions, my judgments, and my relationships; it wasn't a pretty sight. I realized that on any given day, I was sabotaging my own results.

Don't Snooze Through Your Life

Have you ever had one of those mornings when the alarm went off and you immediately hit the snooze bar? Then, of course, you went back to sleep for the best nine minutes of your entire life. The next time the alarm went off, you thought, *I'm not that hungry; I can skip breakfast,* so you reached over and hit the snooze bar again. Nine glorious minutes later, you said to yourself, *I'm clean; no shower today!* and you hit the snooze bar once again. Finally, on the fourth alarm, you grumbled and moaned your way out of bed only to find that you weren't *quite* as clean as you'd hoped and you were ravenous...and now very late!

Can you relate? This was my life! The hardest thing was recognizing that this was just a snapshot of the downward spiral I was living day in and day out. And to think I was actually surprised at my rotten results at the end of each day!

Finally, after enough nagging, disappointment, and stress, I actually listened to the scratching at the back of my mind—I decided I wanted more. I wanted to live as those happy women who seemed to be high on caffeine live. I wanted to be chipper and fun-loving. I wanted to look forward to work. I wanted to be admired by the people around me. I wanted to feel that I was reaching my potential and enjoying my life, every day. I wanted to control my attitude and my results.

Are You Ready to Be a Rhino?

I came to the conclusion that there are really two types of women in this world: those who live their lives like cows, and those who live their lives like rhinos. Too many women live their lives on the sidelines, passively watching everyone else pass them by, much like cows live their lives. They never really make any sudden moves; they just sit and watch everyone else get what they want. I'm convinced that many of them are waiting for something—probably a cowboy—to come along and change the direction of their life. But ultimately, these cows just sit and wait, and wait, and wait.

Then there are those women who live their lives aggressively, like rhinos. Now, cows and rhinos are almost identical physically, with the obvious exception of the enormous snout on the rhino! But consider the muscle and strength of the rhino. Think of its thick skin—everything just rolls off it's back. The rhino sets it's sights, it moves toward what it desires, it takes what it wants, and it does *not* take no for an answer.

That is what living is about: living with purpose, recognizing your values, and creating movement. I want to live my life's purpose and celebrate my values with that same drive, that same passion. How do you want to live *your* life?

Sisters, We Have Arrived!

There is a phenomenon happening in our corporate culture that has never been seen before: Women who have climbed to top positions, with exorbitant salaries, corner offices, never-ending perks, and cushy titles, are leaving the corporate world at alarming rates. The media is actually calling it a "tragic phenomenon"—they claim these women are throwing in the towel because they can't handle the pressure.

These women have chosen to live their lives like rhinos.

For the first time in history, women are finally finding their voices, finally finding their wings. We are realizing that we have more choices now than we ever dreamed possible. For so many years, we have had the tools, we have had the drive, and we certainly have had the vision, but many of us were waiting for just the right opportunity.

Now, finally, women are taking their stand. Women, for the first time, are being given opportunities that were never expected even 30 years ago. We are realizing that we must commit to finding our purpose, whatever that may be.

It is time to paint our own masterpieces. We must find the courage to create a life of vibrant fuchsias, electric blues, and brilliant limes. For too long, we have deliberated over the right brush, the perfect hue, the best lighting. For too long, we have waited for something more, something that we thought was just out of reach. This is our divine canvas...so paint! We must paint with passion, paint with zest, paint with conviction, paint with our hearts. We must paint whatever brings us joy!

This beautiful phenomenon taking place in our corporate culture is about women creating their fulfillment. Women are founding businesses at twice the rate of men—and being twice as successful! More women are going to college, more women are claiming white-collar jobs, and more women are in control of family finances. There are more women running companies, as well as countries, than there ever were in the past.

This is a time of celebration, and a call to action. Women, find your courage and tighten your resolve. Set your sights on what you dreamed of as a little girl. Rise up and break a few rules—then create new ones of your own. Resolve that there is no limit to what you can do and no cap on success. You must recognize an exhilarating fact: You have arrived.

Reclaim Your Destiny

On June 23, 1940, a baby girl named Wilma Rudolph was born three months premature in a shack in the hills of Tennessee. At the age of 4, she contracted pneumonia, scarlet fever, and polio, all at the same time. Though she recovered, doctors assured her family she would never be able to walk again without the use of braces.

She wore her braces for five years, just as she was instructed, but was determined to walk without them. At age 9, Wilma started practicing without her braces. In an amazingly short time, she was walking, just like everyone else. At age 13, Wilma decided that she wanted to be a runner. She entered her first race, certain that she would win, but came in dead last. She entered another race a week later...and came in last again.

Wilma Rudolph kept running and refused to quit. Years later, in front of 80,000 fans, Wilma Rudolph—the little girl born in a shack in the hills of Tennessee, crippled at age 4 and laughed at for trying to walk without braces at age 9—won three gold medals for the United States at the 1960 Olympic Games, the first American woman *ever* to win three gold medals in a single Olympics.

When she was interviewed, everyone wanted to know *why* she ran. Was it for the gold medals? Her country? The accolades? She claimed that she ran simply because she was not going to let anyone else determine her destiny.

Who has determined *your* destiny? Are you living the life you dreamed about as a bright-eyed little girl who knew no boundaries? Does your heart sing wildly when you work? Are you thoroughly enjoying your master plan? If not, what's next? Have you allowed yourself to dream big? Have you allowed yourself to be a little crazy and throw caution to the wind?

When was the last time you dared to create animals in passing clouds like you did as a child? When was the last time you got excited about your life? When was the last time you risked it all to create the life of your childhood dreams?

Imagine what you could create if only you dared to rise up and take a chance!

There Are Only So Many Tomorrows

Eugene Orowitz was a wiry little teenager who was constantly made fun of for his lack of coordination and athletic ability. He was also incredibly shy and self-conscious, which only added to his humiliation. One day, while sitting on the sidelines and observing the high school track team practice, the coach jokingly asked "Ugy" to come and try the javelin. Everyone expected him to make a fool of himself.

Instead, he threw farther than the varsity javelin thrower. He was a natural! From that day on, Ugy practiced diligently. By the time he graduated, he held the national high school record and landed a full college scholarship—he had big dreams of being an Olympic competitor.

Injured, he never made it to the Olympics, but instead of giving up, he decided to chase a new goal—becoming an actor. We now know Eugene Orowitz as Michael Landon, television superstar.

Three weeks before he died, Landon was interviewed in *TV Guide*. "Somebody should tell us, right at the start of our lives, that we are dying," he mused. "Then we might live life to the limit—every minute of every day. Do whatever you want to do. Do it now! There are only so many tomorrows."

Now is the time to rise up and determine what it is that you value in life. I am convinced that many of us are truly unaware of what we value most. So many of us have been running in random directions, putting out fires, doing for others, and taking what we can get at the end of the day. At this pace, we will never create ultimate fulfillment in our lives, because our lives don't fully belong to us. It is time for all of us to enjoy the gift of life that we have been given.

We were all given a wake-up call the dreadful morning of September 11th, and the message we should have received is that nothing in life is guaranteed. We cannot afford to sit around waiting for someone else to change our lives or for something better to come along. This amazing ride we are on has got to be enjoyed to its fullest. Let's not waste our tickets any longer.

Steps to Finding Fulfillment

The first step to creating a fulfilling life is to acknowledge that you not only want more, but that you *deserve* more.

The second step is to establish what you value most. Many of us have never allowed ourselves to determine what we truly value in life because we have been so busy nurturing everyone else's values. As women, we tend to buy into the fear of being called selfish for putting our values first. We've got martyrdom covered, don't we? Remember, if we're not being good to ourselves, we can't possibly be good to other people. It is time to place a high value on what we want, need, and enjoy in life. It is time to create a life of fulfillment!

Following is a list of words describing some of those things we value. Go through it and circle the words that either mean something to you or describe you (or that you *want* to describe you). Circle as many as you like—let your heart make the decisions. Don't judge, second guess, or shame yourself. Just simply recognize those things in your life that you already consider important.

Abundance	Community	Excellence
Acceptance	Compassion	Exhilaration
Accomplish	Complete	Experiment
Action	Conceive	Expert
Acquire	Connection	Facilitate
Admiration	Contentment	Fame
Adventure	Control	Family
Amusement	Courage	Freedom
Arousing	Danger	Friendship
Artistic	Daring	Fun
Assist	Dedication	Gamble
Attain	Delight	Glamour
Attentive	Dependable	Grace
Attractive	Design	Gratitude
Aware	Devotion	Greatest
Beautiful	Direct	Guiding
Blissful	Drama	Health
Bonding	Dream	Holy
Brave	Educate	Honesty
Build	Elegance	Honor
Calm	Encouragement	Humility
Capable	Energize	Humor
Coach	Enjoy	Imagination
Comfort	Enlightenment	Impact
Communication	Entertaining	Improvement

Influence
Informative
Ingenuity
Inspiring
Instruct
Integrity
Invent
Joy
Laughter
Learn
Love
Loyalty
Magnificence
Marriage
Mastery
Mentor
Minister
Model
Observant
Open-minded
Opportunistic
Orchestrate
Originality
Out-do
Passion
Patience
Peaceful
People
Perfection
Perseverance

Persistence
Persuasive
Planner
Playful
Pleasure
Prepared
Prevailing
Provide
Radiance
Relate to God
Relationships
Religious
Resilience
Responsible
Risk
Romance
Rule
Satisfaction
Score
Security
Seeking
Sensational
Sensitivity
Sensual
Serenity
Serve
Sex
Sincere
Spirit
Spirituality

Spontaneity
Sports
Stimulate
Strength
Superiority
Supportive
Tenderness
Thoughtful
Thrill
To contribute
To create
To discover
To experience
To feel
To lead
To nurture
To relate
To teach
To unite
To win
Touch
Triumph
Trustworthy
Truth
Understand
Uplift
Wealth
Win-over
Work

Now that you have gone through the list and circled all of those things that you value, I want you to narrow the list down to just 15 words. Take your time with this step. So often, we place a high value on items that aren't necessarily that important in the grand scheme of things. Having many areas of value in life is not a bad thing, but sometimes our focus gets clouded because we're being pulled in so many directions. When our values aren't clear, we tend to take anything appealing that comes along, getting caught up in "okay" and missing out on "outstanding" because our values have not been clearly defined.

Done? Okay, now that you have identified your top 15 values, I want you to narrow them down to five. This may be difficult, but it is the most important part. To create fulfillment and success in your life, you must have a very clear view of what you are moving toward. Understanding what you value most in life should be liberating and empowering. It should give you direction, clarity, and purpose.

The final step in building a fulfilling life is creating movement. The only thing keeping you from what you want in life is positive movement. You can sit around and think about what you want, complain about not having it, and plan until you are blue in the face, but until you decide to create positive movement, you will not be any closer to your divine purpose. Quiet your fears and put those nagging voices to rest.

You are not defined by what has happened in the past, and no matter how much time you spend dwelling on what has occurred, you will not change the outcome. Let it be; let it go. And don't allow yourself to worry and fret about the future—the "what-ifs" of life. What will be, will be. Regardless of how much time you spend stressing about the future, you will still not be able to control it. Live in the present and seize this glorious moment!

Do You Know Where You're Going?

In the 1920s, Florence Chadwick was determined to be the first woman to swim the English Channel from England to France. Of course, her critics thought it would be impossible for a woman to participate in a race that would take 18 hours or longer to complete. They said that she simply wasn't strong enough.

On the day of the race, Florence had primed her mind and body. She was prepared for victory. After hours of swimming, a heavy fog settled on the edge of the water. The fog was so thick that the swimmers couldn't even see their own hands entering the water, just inches from their noses. After hours of battling the elements, Florence's resolve started to give way. Here was a woman who was ready for this race—prepared mentally and physically. And yet suddenly, her mind started to play tricks on her. She started thinking that she was swimming in circles and must have been going in the wrong direction. She had to be pulled out of the water.

Within moments of being pulled into the boat, Florence discovered that she had been less than 30 yards from the finish line.

The very next year, Florence Chadwick entered the race again. Not deterred by her past failure, she was committed to fulfilling her goal. It was a perfect day for a race: not a cloud in the sky. Within 16 hours, Florence Chadwick became the first woman to swim across the English Channel.

The media, of course, remembered her failure the year before. What had she done differently? How had she turned failure into victory?

Her answer was simple: "I could clearly see the finish line. I knew where I was going."

Do you know where *you* are going? Are you willing to let go of the past, and live in the moment to create positive movement? Like Florence Chadwick, we must have a very clear vision of our finish line in order to create success on any level. When you see your finish line, what obstacles are in your way? What do you need to change in your life in order to guarantee success in this process? Do you need to work on your relationships? Your education? Your finances? Yourself?

Change on any level takes a great amount of discipline and can be a painful process. Change forces us to confront our deep-rooted fears: *What am I going to lose? How painful will it be? What if I fail?* Because we are overly focused on failure, past or future, we literally talk ourselves out of positive movement in the present moment.

Change is exhilarating and healthy. It keeps us alert and on the cutting edge. It creates growth and stimulation. As you decide to change your life, there will certainly be unexpected "hiccups" along the way, but that's what life is about. Funny thing about hiccups: The more you focus on them, the worse they seem to get; they disappear only when you start to relax and realize you can't control them.

That's exactly how change is. It can be annoying and may seem to take forever to get through. But once you relax and go with the flow, you will realize that it really wasn't so bad in the first place. So much of what we stress about in life isn't even going to be remembered in five years...or sometimes five minutes. Setbacks will occur, but stay focused on the prize—this is your life.

It's Not Over Till It's Over

Nicolo Paganini was one of the greatest violinists who ever lived. As he was preparing to put on his final performance in the mid-19th century, people traveled from far and wide to see the Master one last time. The theater was packed with admirers. In the middle of an early passage, Paganini broke one of his strings. The people in the first two rows noticed that the string was dangling, but Paganini never missed a beat. He quickly adjusted his hand on the three remaining strings and continued to play. The majority of the audience did not notice a thing.

As he continued to play with incredible passion, Paganini broke a second string. Now everyone in the audience could see that, in fact, there were two strings hanging from the violin. The crowd started to murmur, wondering what would happen to the show. Paganini stepped to the edge of the stage, raised his hand, and said, "Please! Paganini is not finished." He raised his violin, adjusted his hand on the two remaining strings, and continued to play.

The audience was stunned as they watched him play with a strength and conviction they had never seen in previous performances. Paganini played on. In the middle of another song, he broke a third string. The audience was devastated. They started to talk loudly and grabbed their belongings to exit the theater. The Maestro realized he was losing control. He grabbed a chair from the corner of the stage, slammed it down, then jumped onto it and screamed at the top of his lungs for all to hear, "Please! Paganini is not finished!"

He raised his violin and adjusted his hand on the last remaining string. From the top of the chair, on one string, Paganini played. He played on that one string for 23 minutes, then purposely broke it.

Paganini was finished.

As you create purpose and fulfillment in your life, I hope you live passionately like the rhino. Be brave and focused. Tighten your resolve and set your sights on what will bring you joy. Like Paganini, sometimes your plans will fall apart and your supporters will turn their backs on you. Strengthen your emotional stamina. This is the one shot we have to get it right.

Life is not a spectator sport. The longer we sit back passively, watching and waiting, the longer someone else will be enjoying what we deserve. The only difference between you and those already enjoying what you want is positive movement. So, get ready, get set...GO! Grab at your chance and know that this is your divine right. This is your blank canvas. Live your life with electric blues and vibrant fuchsias— you are the only artist of your glorious masterpiece. Live each day beautifully as if it's your last. Recognize that you have been placed here at this moment to reflect on the gift that you have been given, and ultimately to create a new path: a path of love, laughter, excitement, and fulfillment.

Remember, like Paganini, you have so much left to play!

The Dash

By Alton Maiden

I've seen death stare at me with my own eyes in a way many cannot know
I've seen death take others, but still left me below
I've heard many scream of mother's cries but death refuses to hear
In my life I've seen faces fill with many tears.

After death has come and gone a tombstone sits for many to see
But it is no more than a symbol of a person's memory
I've seen my share of tombstones but never took the time to truly read
The meaning behind what is there for others to see.

Under the person's name it read the date of birth-Dash-and the date the
person passed
But the more I think about the tombstone, the important thing is the Dash
Yes, I see the name of the person but that I might forget
I also read the date of birth and death but even that might not stick.

But thinking about the individual, I can't help but remember the Dash
Because it represents a person's life and that will always last
So when you begin to charter your life make sure you're on a positive path
Because people may forget your birth and death
But they will never forget your Dash.

♦ ♦ ♦

* This is a poem that football coach Lou Holtz reads at many of his speaking engagements. Alton Maiden played football at Notre Dame in the mid-1990s (when Holtz was the coach).

♦ ♦ ♦

Jennifer Buck Curtet's energy and passion have won her rave reviews from audiences across the country, many of whom claim she is "the most motivational speaker we ever heard—absolutely amazing!" Her information-rich seminars are packed with practical, real-world skills and tempered with her own engaging mixture of warmth and humor. Jennifer is a master storyteller.

Jennifer spent a decade as a trainer and manager for Morgan Stanley Dean Witter. She was responsible for writing, developing, and delivering training programs that are still required for all levels of leadership at the company.

Through her company, Aristocrat Enterprises, Jennifer is hired for keynotes, conferences, and training seminars to industry leaders throughout the world. Her clients include Coca-Cola, Johnson & Johnson, Wal-Mart, Western Union, Cisco Systems, PricewaterhouseCoopers, the Department of Defense, Bank One, Andrews Air Force Base, Hampton University, Johns Hopkins University, and the State of Missouri.

A devoted mentor, Jennifer has been a speaker for the Make-A-Wish Foundation.

Jennifer's passion and persistence have inspired hundreds of thousands of women across the country to rise up and fulfill their destinies. United, she proclaims, women are unstoppable!

Contact Jennifer and Aristocrat Enterprises via the Internet at *www.Aristocratenterprises.com*, via e-mail at Jennifer@Aristocratenterprises.com, or by phone at 602-421-8653.

Pam Royle

It's Never Too Late to Let Go

I'm a collector...I collect *stuff*...I treasure it, absorb it, feel it, can't part with it, pack-rat it, stuff it, save it...and never deal with it.

I've saved string, old shoes, children's pictures, toys, books, and games. Baskets of audio tapes with sounds of children laughing, quartets singing, speeches resonating.

I still have my children's arts and crafts projects from grade school—you know, the ones that look like owls, made by inking thumb prints on small stones and then painting in the eyes (spooky but effective).

I have programs from long-lost theater productions, strands of jewelry that my mother wore, broken Christmas ornaments that still have a memory attached.

· And the truth of the matter is I CAN'T LET any of it GO! I save it. I collect it. But I can't *deal* with it!

Thirty years ago, my husband and I moved into a new home in St. Louis. We unpacked everything, except for a few boxes that we stacked in a back corner of the basement. As they were clearly marked "Misc. Stuff," they were obviously not critical to our new life. So there they sat...and sat...and *sat*, accumulating dust; out of sight, out of mind.

Thirty years later, they remain where they were placed, unopened, unremembered, unmissed. With the wisdom age has given me, I'm now *afraid* to open them. I've lived without whatever mysteries they contain for 30 years, but I know that once opened, I'll find some long-lost treasure that I simply won't be able to part with.

Oh, I forgot I had that! How lovely! So glad I found this again; it brings back so many memories.

And back in the box it will go, to be stored, saved and forgotten for another 30 years.

My children are resigned to the fact that at some point *they'll* have to deal with my "collections."

Good thing Mom isn't here. She'd have a fit if she saw us pitching, stomping, and trashing her "stuff." What in the world was she thinking? What is all this anyway?

Well, the stuff is just...*stuff,* inanimate objects that bring joy to the person who remembers them and what they "mean," useless to those who can't make the connection. A baby's first toy is a memory for the mother, not for the child. And a hand-knit afghan is just a blanket...unless you were there to see arthritic fingers struggling with the yarn, laboring long hours to give a gift of love. Letting go of these things—this *stuff*—is, in the long run, painful. It is not impossible.

But there are other collectibles not so easily dismissed. Over the years I've also collected old wounds, bad memories, unhappy moments, opportunities lost, relationships destroyed. They fester inside and, in moments of dark despair, are taken out and revisited, as if by doing so they could be transformed into pleasant memories of happier times.

How do we let go of *these* things? How and where do we discard these living, breathing emotions that kill our insides and destroy our confidence and self-esteem? Where can we store guilt, envy, disappointment, anger, and unhappiness? We certainly can't just box them up and hide them in a corner of the basement. Wherever we go, whoever we become, we carry them with us, letting them negatively affect our minds and bodies.

And where do we *learn* this other "stuff"—the thoughts and feelings that declare we're not worthy, not important, not pretty, not necessary, not talented, not valuable? The stuff that takes away our power and leaves us with insecurities that stifle our creativity?

Surprisingly enough, much of it comes from people who love us, those who certainly wish us no harm. As a very wise person once said, "We are what we hear at the top of the stairs…when our parents don't think we're listening."

One of my early dreams was to play the piano. I begged and begged until eventually my parents found $50 to buy an old, raggedy upright piano, and I began my lessons. I banged and pounded and practiced and loved every minute of it. One day as I was playing, my mother had a friend over to visit.

"My, Pam certainly loves playing that piano, doesn't she?" my mother's friend remarked.

"Yes," replied my mother. "She'll never be very good, but she does love to play."

I stopped practicing. To this day, I can only plunk and plod through the simplest of melodies. My mother loved me dearly, and I'm sure she never knew how discouraged I was by her remark. She was probably only stating the truth—a truth perhaps colored by her own insecurities and my painful rendition of "Nola" —but it hurt nonetheless. To this day, I find myself giving up when I recognize that other people seem to be able to do things easier or better because, as my mother said, "Pam will never be very good." That's what my mother actually *said*. What I *heard* was, "Pam will never be *good enough*."

And so begins the collection of mental "stuff." It gets stored in the drawers and closets of our minds and shapes the image of our place in the universe. Somewhere inside, we all face the demons of self-worth and wonder if people will see beyond the false faces we present to the world and discover that we're really not worthy.

I've let so many opportunities go by over the years because I "wasn't good enough."

My mother told me so.

I had my own radio show at the age of 17, "Tunes for Teens." I loved it. The station manager encouraged me to fill out an application for *McCall's* magazine, which, at the time, was doing a feature on teenagers who were "making a difference."

No thanks. That wasn't me. My mother told me so.

In college I was offered a job at the local radio station. I turned it down; I said I didn't have a car. The truth was, I just wasn't good enough.

My mother told me so.

As an adult, I've needed constant validation, even from my children, that I'm capable, exceptional, and better than "*summa cum* average." I'm harder on myself than anybody has a right to be. Because I need to prove that I really *am* good enough.

The ego is a delicate thing, and negative input is so powerful that it attaches to our persona as easily as magnets to a refrigerator. We start our collection of tapes at an early age—the tapes that say "I'm not good enough" or "I'm not capable enough"—and keep playing them in our heads throughout adulthood. As a result, we diminish our power to excel.

I'm not atypical of my generation. Many of us went straight from high school to college to marriage, never experiencing a chance to spread our wings and fly, except under somebody else's tutelage, by somebody else's rules; never a time to test our abilities, overcome our fears, prove that we really did have what it takes.

And it's not just my generation of women. It's enlightening and sometimes hilarious to watch the 10 o'clock news and listen to high-performance athletes—strong, tall warriors in full battle gear—talking about "getting their confidence back." "We've got to start believing in ourselves again," they say. "We've got to go out tomorrow night and do what we know we can do." And I'm reassured, knowing that if the strongest and mightiest among us can suffer from self-doubt, I'm probably not doing too badly.

The truth is, my mother never told me I wasn't good enough. My mother loved me and supported me and took great pride in all of my accomplishments. But somewhere in the back of my mind was that little tiny voice that wanted me to *believe* I'm not good enough.

The "not good enough" syndrome was the first step in a journey of insecurity that ended in guilt and a lifetime of looking back and "shoulding" on myself: I *should* have been a better mother! I *should* have read more stories to my children. I *should* have spent more time with each of them. I *should* have listened more. I *should* have fixed better meals.

I should have made different choices. I shouldn't have married so young, had children so late, worked so hard, allowed so many people to push me around.

I should have taken better care of my mother. She was so lonely after my dad died. I lived too far away, and it was hard to find ways to deal with her pain, so I shut her out. I never called her on Sundays when I knew she was alone. And when she called me, and I could hear the loneliness in her voice and the tears in her eyes, I found excuses—places I had to go, people I needed to see, children I had to take care of. Anything to end the conversation.

It's *my fault* my son has asthma—if I hadn't been a smoker, he might have been a healthier child. My daughter might have been a ballerina—if I had taken more time off to drive her to ballet class. My son might have been a singer if I'd beaten up the teacher who told him he sang like a girl. My marriage might have lasted if I hadn't been an enabler, if I'd had more sense than brains.

Flog! Flog! Pity! Pity! It's time to beat up on the Ego and the Id again.

This was my life, this was my inner being, this was my essence for the vast majority of my lifetime.

But then a strange thing happened. I woke up on the morning of my 62nd birthday and had an epiphany. Lightening struck in that moment between darkness and dawn—I realized that my "some days" were shorter than they used to be. You know, the places you're going to go "some day," the things you're going to do "some day," the books you're going to read, the hobbies you're going to start, the promises you're going to keep. Well, there just weren't as many "some days" left!

My life, I realized, had simply *happened*, flowing like a river through the countryside, invariably taking the path of least resistance. I had never thought forward, only looked back. I'd never planned, never set goals, never had expectations beyond the "some day I'm gonna" kind.

I knew that morning that if I wanted things to be different, I'd better get up and get going. I'd better make some serious life changes or the river would continue to flow past opportunities and dreams, and I might never see them again. I'd lived my life with either regrets for things not done or promises of "some days" to come. It was time to make some changes.

I started by writing down all the things I'd accomplished in my life, things that seemed to be just happy accidents and side trips down my lazy, meandering river:

- ◆ I raised three beautiful children who have turned into fine adults. They're not singers or dancers, but they're happy, healthy, fairly well-adjusted...and anything more is now their responsibility.

- ◆ I started a repertoire company that produced neighborhood variety shows for more than 20 years. I thought this was just for fun, but now I know it was an integral part in developing my people skills and management style.

- ◆ I built a healthcare company from startup to $3 million in sales. True, I started as a file clerk because my husband said he needed some clerical help in the office, but 20 years later, I was the company's Administrative Director, running nine offices in the state of Missouri and overseeing nine branch managers, 10 nurses, 300 caregivers, and 600 clients.

- ◆ I worked on legislation that helped supply home care to thousands of Missouri's frail, elderly, and disabled population.

- ◆ I founded a chorus that now numbers more than 100 women, has performed at Walt Disney World, competed internationally with the Sweet Adelines organization for almost 25 years, and is recognized as one of its premier choruses.

- ◆ I sang in a competitive barbershop quartet that was once ranked 17th in the world. (And it's okay that we never won first place or even cracked the top 10.)

◆ I served on a variety of boards; counseled numerous friends through births, deaths, divorce, and depression; befriended the friendless; and did what I could to make the world a little better than when I found it.

When I was finished with my list, I realized I hadn't done such a bad job after all. It wasn't all sunshine and lollypops, but it was, without a doubt, "good enough."

I gave myself permission to let go, to "whoosh" it all out of my system, and to begin all over again on an exciting new journey. Since that wonderful morning, I've begun to actually live, to grab those "some days" I was going to have. I'm traveling and teaching and taking every opportunity to share my stories with as many women as will listen. I talk to them about planning, about being kind to themselves, about traveling forward and not looking back. And I have better talks with myself now, talks that boost my ego instead of tearing it down. I've become my own best friend, and I like me, I really do!

This past year I attended the Sweet Adelines International convention in Nashville. The Sweet Adelines sing beautifully, but they sleep cheap, so I had three roommates to contend with. Donna, the fastest of the bunch, beat me to the shower the first morning. She came out laughing and said, "Pam, when you get out of the shower, look on the mirror. If you don't see anything, I'll know it was meant for me." After I'd showered, the mirror was covered with steam. At the top you could see where someone had written, "Humble, but gorgeous!" I laughed, of course, and then I got to thinking, "What if everyone stepped out of the shower in the morning and was reminded of their power, their worth, their beauty? And then it struck me...another epiphany: I could plant the seeds of self-worth just by writing on mirrors. Now, as I travel, I leave every hotel room just a little bit better than when I found it. I leave hidden messages in the steam for some unsuspecting soul to read when he or she steps out of the shower. I hope it brings them a smile and a reminder that they're wonderful.

I still collect "stuff," but now I concentrate on new friends, new places, and new ideas. Every day I look for ways to give myself positive self-affirmations: *I really did that well; I look especially nice today; I'm not just "good enough," I'm GREAT!*

Life without guilt, life without doubt, is a wonder. I'm 65 and living my dreams. The kids are gone; the dog is dead, and I am movin' on!

Dynamic, upbeat, and fun are three words that audiences have used to describe Pam Royle.

Arriving in Chicago from a small town in Michigan, Pam turned from teaching to television and soon began a successful career working for WTTW, Chicago's PBS station. She also kept her teaching skills sharp as an instructor for a Chicago secretarial college teaching both business English and typing.

Pam moved to St. Louis, Missouri in the 1970s. She raised three children, founded a 100-plus women's a capella chorus (now ranked 12th in the world), developed a repertoire theater company that entertained thousands of enthusiastic supporters for more than 20 years, and was instrumental in developing a secretarial training program for a St. Louis-based technical school. Pam became their first instructor in business English.

In the early 80s, Pam turned her organizational talents to the successful development of a home-care agency. It soon became one of Missouri's largest home-care providers, with offices stretching from Iowa to Arkansas and a staff of 300 caregivers providing direct care to some 600 clients.

In the mid-90s, Pam began PDR Resources, a company dedicated to training home-care management, direct-care staff, and consumers.

Pam is now sharing her experiences with audiences all over the country. Whether the subject is negativity in the work place, dealing with difficult people, team-building, or writing for success, Pam knows first-hand about the problems and the possibilities.

Pam's a "been there, done that" business professional whose biggest thrill is helping others realize the potential of their dreams.

Jana Stanfield

THREE STEPS TO MORE COURAGE

"Whatever you can do, or dream you can, begin it.
Boldness has genius, power, and magic in it."

—Goethe

Is there a dream that keeps you awake nights? A burning urge to change *something, everything*? One so urgent that you feel in your heart you *must* do something about it, or burst?

I *know* that feeling. I had that dream. I acted on it. And today, I'm living it. And in this brief chapter, I can show you how you can build *your* dream, one simple step at a time.

Most of you reading this book already have big commitments to think about—demanding careers, families to support, debts to pay... probably all three. You have invested a great deal of time, energy, and love to get what you have, and there's no way you can throw it all away. You have traveled a long way down your path. Giving up all you've got and starting over is not an option.

Fortunately, there's a better way, one each of you can use, no matter what your situation, your talents or, for that matter, your dream: Start where you are and begin building a bridge. How? By using a process I call "Three Steps, No Failure."

Three Steps, No Failure

I learned this simple but invaluable concept when I was a beginning television news reporter at an NBC affiliate in Albuquerque, New Mexico. With a degree in Broadcasting and the dream of being an entertainer, my intention was to get one year of experience after college. That way, I could always fall back on broadcasting if music—my real dream—didn't work out.

As you might have guessed, that one year became four years quicker than you can say, "Jana Stanfield, *Eyewitness News*." The longer I stayed, the more demanding the job became. I don't want to paint too horrific a picture. There were some enviable perks, too, such as awards, prestige, and trips to cover interesting stories in interesting places. I was recognized at the mall. Some of my stories were sold to the network, and my parents got to see me on *NBC News*. I even was sent to Washington, D.C., to cover the second inauguration of Ronald Reagan.

The awful part was that there were probably thousands of young women all over the country who would have killed to have my job. And I was living it—but I didn't want it.

This career I had stepped into halfheartedly was wrapping its tentacles around me so tightly that I couldn't escape. I kept having this dream that I was hanging from a rope tied to a hot-air balloon that had lifted off and was heading skyward. With every foot that the balloon rose, it increased the chances of me being killed or badly injured if I let go. Caught between the fear of letting go and the fear of holding on, I felt immobilized as the balloon (my job) swept me away to a place I never intended to go. Any of you who are trapped in a career that is far from your dream can relate to this feeling.

My father knew how much I wanted to pursue music, because that had always been *his* dream, too. He understood my feeling of being trapped in my job because I simply had no idea how to make my musical dreams come true...and still support myself. Dad called my uncle, the Reverend Clyde Stanfield, a United Methodist minister and professional counselor. Clyde, who was serving an Albuquerque church across town from the television station, called to see if I'd like to get together for lunch once a week. It was during these wonderful lunches that he taught me "Three Steps, No Failure."

After patiently listening to me for most of the first lunch, Clyde gave me an assignment for the next lunch.

"What we need to do is build a bridge," he said. "You don't have to be able to see the other side yet. You just need to be able to see the first three steps. Once you take those first three steps, you'll be able to see the next three."

The assignment was simple: Make a list of three things you can do in a week that will take you closer to where you want to be. There's only one guideline for choosing the steps: Each one has to be something you couldn't *possibly* fail at in a week's time. In other words, each step had to be short and sweet and eminently doable.

This was my first list:

1. Buy a book about the music business.
2. Call a voice teacher to see how much lessons would cost.
3. Order cable television so I could watch The Nashville Network.

I had been thinking about doing all three of these things, plus many others, for a long time. But I thought that none of these steps, or even all three of them, would make my dream come true, so it felt like useless effort.

Nevertheless, I tried Clyde's method.

The Magic of the First Three Steps

When we can't see the road ahead, it can immobilize us. We can get "caught between fear and faith." When we focus on just walking, one step at a time, instead of worrying about the road ahead, amazing things can happen. Each small set of steps leads logically to the next small set of steps. Before you know it, you're on a journey...and making progress!

It didn't take a genius to figure out that when I showed my list to Clyde, my next week's assignment would simply be to do the things on the list. I was so excited about building this bridge that I not only arrived at our next lunch with the list, but with all three steps accomplished. I felt exhilarated at my accomplishments, and anxious to take three more steps. Here's what evolved from those first three steps.

1. Buy a book.

Each of the three steps will always logically lead to the next three. Once I bought the book, my next step was to set a goal of the number of pages I was certain I could read in a week. I didn't put any pressure on myself to make it a large number. Just making progress felt wonderful! That feeling of progress was so new that it could have been easily shattered by small failures, so I avoided putting anything on my list that I couldn't accomplish easily. Within a few weeks, I had finished reading the book.

2. Call a voice teacher.

For months, I had been thinking of calling Linda Cotton, a wonderful singer in Albuquerque who had her own jazz band and also taught voice. In addition to the hopelessness that kept me from calling her, I also was intimidated by her enormous talent and scared of asking anyone for help. The whole thing made me feel so vulnerable. That's why I didn't list signing up for voice lessons. I would just *inquire* about them.

When I talked to Linda on the phone, I found that her prices were affordable, that the place where she taught was not far from the station, and that she was kind and caring and warm. Right then and there, I took another step: I set up an appointment with her for a lesson.

After the lesson, Linda told me about a gifted piano player, Sid Fendley, who had left her band to play at a local country club. She suggested I call him—my next step. It turned out that Sid was looking for someone to come out on weekends and sing with him in the country club's piano bar. I had a job as a singer!

Meeting Sid turned everything around for me musically. For the first time in my life, making music was more than just a beloved hobby. While still doing the news, I was actually *working* in music (and getting paid for it). Sid was a wonderful mentor who taught me about living the life of a full-time musician, from practice and performance to professionalism and paychecks. With Sid playing piano and me doing most of the singing, we worked together for nearly a year, eventually moving from the country club to a job at a nice downtown hotel where all my friends and even my coworkers at the television station could come to hear us. I loved singing with Sid every weekend. I loved practicing every week. We made good money, and it was a thrill for me to learn the ins and outs of a career in music.

3. Order cable.

What about that third step? After ordering cable, one of the new steps that frequently showed up on my weekly list was to watch two programs on The Nashville Network: *Nashville Now*, a nightly country music talk show, and *You Can Be A Star*, a daily talent contest that awarded a recording contract to the Grand Prize winner. Each episode of *You Can Be A Star* was followed by an announcement that said, "If you'd like to appear on *You Can Be A Star*, simply call this number or write to this address for information." Of course, I put it on my list one week to call for information.

When I contacted the producer, he was very friendly and unpretentious, immediately putting me at ease. He told me everything I needed to know about how to send in a tape to be considered for the show, so I had plenty of little steps to take in the coming weeks. My tape was approved and I was invited to appear. I used my two weeks of vacation time to be on the show, explore the Nashville music scene, and look for a job.

I didn't win the grand prize on the show, but I hit the jackpot with those job interviews. Soon after returning home, I got an offer from one of interviewers, which gave me a job in the music business that paid as much as my job at the television station!

I won't say that every single step of the hundreds I took delivered a miracle. I'm not going to detail the talent contests I entered and lost, the unsuccessful Opryland auditions that I flew to Memphis for that year, or the horrible band I rehearsed with for months and performed with for two weeks. These were some of the *low*lights. Most of it was mundane stuff, putting one foot in front of the other, making plodding progress. It was the progress that I loved, though, even when I was getting home at 3 a.m. from the band gig and getting up at dawn to be in full makeup for my television job. Finally, I had learned how to give myself hope, by practicing three easy steps per week at which I couldn't possibly fail.

Within a year of writing down those first tentative steps, I was living in Nashville and working in the music business. I continued to take three steps a week to achieve my dream of becoming a recording artist. A look at my biography at the end of this chapter (and the lyrics to one of my better-known songs) will give you a pretty good notion of how that came out!

Three Steps, No Failure

1. To remind yourself how brave you are, name three things you've done in your life that took a lot of courage.

2. To reach a goal you've been dreaming of, break it down into the first three tiny steps. The steps have to be *so easy* that you have to be able to accomplish them, even during your busiest week. You don't have to know exactly where you're going or how to get there yet. When (or before) you get to the third baby step, the next three steps will be obvious.

3. Take the easiest step first. As you move forward at a pace of just three baby steps a week, you'll be amazed at how fast you'll make progress.

One Dream at a Time

"Three steps, no failure" is a powerful concept. Each step is building a bridge—very slowly, perhaps, but very surely—to your dream. That's dream, singular. While I'm sure some of you are completely capable of working on more than one dream at a time, may I suggest you stick with one, accomplish it, and then move on to the next?

Let's not even call your goal a "dream," just a project, like a term paper you had to write in college or a presentation you had to prepare for work. This will make the process less intimidating.

Choose the easiest project, or the one that *seems* the easiest. This offers two clear advantages: First, it will get you going and give you the confidence you need to take on a more complicated project later. Second, it will be easier to devise the first three steps and begin to think about where they may lead. When we set goals that are too far away, it's hard to take into account the everyday challenges and commitments of life. It makes it too easy to feel like we're not making any progress if we haven't reached our goal. If we constantly judge ourselves by how far we are from our goals, we will always come up short.

With a goal of one project at a time, you can go at your own pace. You don't have to know what the next project will be. As you are in the process of each project, the next project will present itself to you. You will know what to do, and as you do it, the next project will begin to take shape.

A Final Note of Encouragement

If there is a longing somewhere deep inside you to let your music be heard, pay attention to that longing.

If there is a whisper somewhere deep inside you that is urging you to take a risk, listen to that whisper.

The longing and the whisper are there for a reason. If you pay attention to the longing and listen for the whisper, they will take you where you need to go and teach you what you need to know.

If I Were Brave

By Jana Stanfield and Jimmy Scott

What would I do if I knew that I could not fail?
If I believed would the wind always fill up my sail?
How far would I go, what could I achieve
Trusting the hero in me?

(Chorus)
If I were brave I'd walk the razor's edge
Where fools and dreamers dare to tread
Never lose faith, even when losing my way
What step would I take today if I were brave?

What if we're all meant to do what we secretly dream?
What would you ask if you knew you could have anything?
Like the mighty oak sleeps in the heart of a seed
Are there miracles in you and me?

Repeat Chorus

What would I do today if I were brave?
What would I do today if I were brave?
What would I do today if I were brave?
What would I do today if I were brave?
If I refuse to listen to the voice of fear
Would the voice of courage whisper in my ear?

Repeat Chorus

What would I do today if I were brave?
What would I do today if I were brave?
What would I do today if I were brave?
What would I do today if I were brave?

When Jana Stanfield couldn't get a recording contract with a record company, she did the next best
thing—she started her *own* record company, which
over the past 12 years, has sold more than 100,000
copies of her CDs. Known as "The Queen of Heavy
Mental," Jana calls her music "psychotherapy you can
dance to." You've heard her compositions on *20/20,
Entertainment Tonight, Oprah*, and radio stations
nationwide. With song titles like, "Bitter or Better,"
"I'm Not Lost, I'm Exploring," "What is Mine Will Find
Me," and "What Would I Do Today If I Were Brave,"
her lyrics are playful, heartwarming, and encouraging.

Her song "If I Had Only Known," recorded by Reba
McEntire, sold four million copies, earning her a platinum album. She also has a gold album for writing a
Suzy Boggus song, and another platinum album for a
song on the soundtrack of the movie *8 Seconds*, star-
ring Luke Perry.

When Jana found that concert settings didn't always
give her enough latitude to share the stories that inspired her songs, she entered the world of professional
speaking as a "motivational performer." She turned
her show into a "Keynote Concert" and began sharing her music and message at conferences and con-
ventions throughout the country.

At a conference or in concert, Stanfield is warm and
humorous, with an enthralling voice that's reminis-
cent of Jewel, Judy Collins, or Joni Mitchell. She's
opened for fellow artists ranging from The Dixie Chicks
to Kenny Loggins.

To explore bringing Jana Stanfield's Keynote Concert
to your group, call: 1-888-530-JANA.

Jan Elliott

MAKE YOUR VOCATION YOUR VACATION

"If you do what you love, you will never work another day in your life."
—Michael Nolan

Let me get right to the point: The secret of success is making your vocation your vacation. In other words, one way to have passion in your life is to do what you love and to love what you do.

I am fortunate to be able to say that I love what I do. My personal mission statement reads: "There is no greater occupation in the world than to assist another human being—to help someone succeed." I am privileged to present seminars, training, and keynote speeches to many different groups of people almost every day. To be able to motivate and inspire someone to reach their personal best or to set higher goals gives me passion for what I do every day.

But maybe you are not as fortunate. Maybe you are anything *but* passionate about your job or career. Maybe you just ended up there. Maybe you don't see a way out.

Maybe you just never looked.

Dr. John C. Maxwell has described three types of job-holders:

1. *Those who don't know what they'd like to do.* These people have no clue. They just get up in the morning without much of a plan of action and float through the day.

2. *Those who know what they would like to do, but just don't do it.* When asked what they would like to do, they can tell you. Why don't they do it? You've never heard so many excuses!

3. *Those who are doing what they want to do.* They are fulfilled, they are passionate, and they are making significant, positive contributions to their own lives and the lives of others.

Here's how to become the third kind of person.

Develop Your Strengths

"To build on a person's strengths, that is, to enable him to do what he can do, will make him effective...to try to build on his weaknesses will be...frustrating and stifling."

—*Peter Drucker*

So, how do your go about doing what you love and loving what you do?

First, you must build on your strengths (whatever comes easily for you). List each attribute or skill you consider a strength. Then rate each on a scale of 1 to 10, with 10 being the strongest. Be honest. *Really* honest. If you are having trouble, ask a friend to help you list or rate your strengths.

If one of your strengths is a 6 or a 7, what would it take to make it a 10? People pay for 10s! Do you need more training? Should you go back to school? Just need more practice? How much time do you have or are you willing to devote to developing this strength? Do you know someone who is doing what you want to do? Would you be willing to invite that person to lunch to learn the real ins and outs of what you want to do with that strength?

After successfully completing a weight loss program, I was invited to take an entry-level position as a counselor. I eventually worked my way up to Regional Trainer. I had to overcome many obstacles to succeed. I had never been a Center Director, but I was expected to train Center Directors. I learned how. I worked with a supervisor who was much younger than I, someone who had a very different value system. I struggled—every day—for a long time.

But I loved what I did! I trained new employees to become consultants, taught them how to motivate and support clients. I later took on even more responsibility as the Assistant Regional Director, which added management duties to my training responsibilities. I truly liked going to work every day.

Then, one day, it was announced that my Regional Supervisor would be receiving a promotion to Divisional Supervisor. After much thought, discussion, and many questions, it was decided that I would be promoted to the Regional Director position. I would no longer motivate new and existing employees; rather, I would be responsible for the bottom line.

After about six months, I was no longer passionate about my position and the company. I was no longer doing what I loved every day. I lasted another long, long six months and then decided to make a change. I resigned. I felt as though someone had died. I had thought I would work for that company forever. But my strengths were in motivation, enthusiasm, speaking, and training—and I no longer got to use them.

Are You Ready To Work Hard?

Second, do you truly have the desire to make it happen? The tenacity? The perseverance? It won't happen overnight. Do you have the patience to work on your strength to make it a 10? How long will it take? A month? A year? Longer? If you are truly passionate about doing what you love and loving what you do, it will be worth the time you have to put into it.

I had been taking graduate classes towards a certificate in training and development, but going back to Corporate America was not what I wanted. I wanted to be a speaker and seminar leader. So, after my resignation, I attended a motivational time-management seminar. Yep, that was what I wanted to do! I wanted to be that speaker!

I had always done some speaking to business associations and church functions. But could I really get good enough so that people would *pay* to hear me speak? Well, I began working for a small training company. I watched many videos of professional speakers and trainers, studying how they moved across the stage, how they used hand gestures or voice inflections. What they wore. How they presented themselves.

I gradually had opportunities to speak for larger seminar companies. Yes, people were actually willing to pay to hear me speak! I can clearly remember the first speaking engagement I gave that paid much more than seminar companies paid. I was elated. They paid me for doing something that I had so much passion to do.

Build the Right Attitude

Finally, do you have the right attitude? As Zig Ziglar says, "Stinkin' thinkin' won't get you anywhere." Change your attitude and you can change your life. What messages are you sending yourself? What conversations are you having inside your head? Wise King Saul once wrote, "As a man thinks, so he becomes." Change those messages to yourself and start setting goals and believing you CAN do it. I know you've read that before. But do you believe it?

After many of my seminars, not all of my evaluations were perfect. At first, I was offended. Who did they think they were? Well, they were my audience! When even one of my marks was not perfect, I listened to what the participant had to say. But first I had to change my attitude about it, to be open to feedback, be open to someone else's perspective. Then I had to work on relationships with others, because, as John Maxwell noted, "people won't *go* along with you if they can't *get* along with you."

Doing what you love and loving what you do will generate the passion you've been missing. Give it all you've got. Turning that vocation into your daily vacation may be the best thing you have ever done to create passion in your life.

Go ahead, what are you waiting for? Live and work passionately!

When you know what you want and you want it badly enough, you will find the ways to get it. That passion is like the gas in your car: Without it, you won't get very far. Find your strengths, make them the best they can be, add passion, and the road ahead will be the shortest route to your life's fulfillment.

Happy traveling!

Jan Elliott is a dynamic speaker and educator who gains immense satisfaction from coaching, mentoring, and guiding others to achieve their "personal best." Jan has earned high praise as a seminar leader for her empowering, idea-focused programs. She presents more than 200 programs and keynotes around the country every year, providing a dose of humor mixed with specific tools and strategies to improve performance.

Her solid background in business skills and management training served her well as a regional supervisor/trainer for a major weight management corporation. In this position, she was responsible for management training in the areas of sales, supervision, performance, motivation, time-management, training/facilitation skills, and staff development. Prior to this position, she founded her own interior design consulting business—Innovative Interiors—where she learned first-hand the value of excellent customer service, one-on-one communication, and effective time-management.

Jan may be reached through her Website, *www.janspeaks.com.*

Candy Whirley

BECOMING THE PERSON YOU CHOOSE TO BE

It was August 1980, a sultry summer day. My mother and I slowly sat down side by side on the steps outside my doctor's office. I remember it as if it were yesterday—we couldn't make it back to the car, we *had* to talk right then.

"Mom, I don't know what to do. I can't believe this happened to me, *me* of all people!"

She held my hand, gently but tightly. "We'll get through this," she said.

"But I don't know if I can go through with it!"

Her next words have been seared into my heart to this day: "You will *not* get rid of my first grandchild!"

As I write these words, the emotions I felt so keenly more than 20 years ago are still in my heart and soul. I used to refer to experiences, especially unpleasant ones, as life's "hiccups." Well, this was one major hiccup!

You see, I was Daddy's little girl—the homecoming candidate, the beauty pageant contestant, the Kansas City Chiefs Chiefette! I was the princess of the family, the only girl and the oldest child, with three younger brothers. I was the leader, the mentor, the never-do-wrong sister and daughter. My mother and father had been happily married for 18 years (now 41). We had the perfect life.

I had already decided I wanted to be a professional dancer on Broadway or in Las Vegas. I received a scholarship from one of my beauty pageants and applied it towards UMKC Conservatory of Dance, a local university in Kansas City. Two weeks into my college career, I started not feeling well during my ballet classes. Actually, I hadn't felt well for several weeks. My Grandma lived right down the street, and I would go to her apartment to take naps in between classes. I started to notice that the ill feeling was in my stomach and that it was usually worse in the morning.

That's when I knew my life had changed, my hopes and dreams shattered.

I was 17 years old, single, and pregnant.

Choose Your Attitude

"Everything can be taken from a man but one thing,
the last of the human freedoms—to choose one's attitude in any given
set of circumstances, to choose one's own way."

—*Victor Frankl*

Has life ever thrown you a complete curveball, taken you down a path totally different than the one you were expecting? What did you do, or what are you doing about it right now? Most important, what was your attitude?

Life has a funny way of flinging challenges our way, and our attitude toward these challenges has much to do with what we learn and who we become. We are *all* going to experience those hiccups, and we need to have an optimistic attitude to get through those difficult times in our lives.

Of course, some of us have bigger hiccups to deal with than others. And it's easy to just say, "Hey, have a positive attitude and everything will be better." So let's talk about the practical tools you can use to develop the attitude you want and, by extension, the life you want.

After a recent seminar I gave about the importance of attitude, a participant I'll call Betty ran up to me and said, "Candy, I was just diagnosed with Attention Deficit Disorder (ADD) and I am *so* excited!"

I was pretty puzzled about her reaction until she explained: For most of her life, everyone had told her she was stupid; teachers had written on her report card that she was a difficult child; she was punished by teachers and by her parents because of her inattentiveness. Although her life had been far from easy, Betty never gave up—her attitude was one of optimism and hope. The payoff happened when she was diagnosed, as an adult, with ADD. The doctor put her on medication, she went back to college, got her degree, and even graduated at the top of her class!

Betty could have had a pessimistic attitude, could have given up, and never found out that her problem was a simple chemical imbalance, a *correctable* imbalance. She could have listened to those people in her life and told herself, "They're right. I am worthless. I am stupid," until she believed it.

But she didn't.

I hope you adopt her positive outlook. I am not naive. I know that we *all* have those times when we want to just give up...but we can't. We have to develop a "can-do" attitude like Betty, to get through those *hiccups*.

I have a special technique I use when these *hiccups* happen to me. It's an easy acronym to remember: **CAN**—**C**hange **A**ttitude **N**ow. Here's how it works:

Take a minute and think about the three most important things in your life right now—objects, memories, or people. Write them down on a sheet of paper.

The next time you are feeling that you can't take another *hiccup* in your life, I want you to think about whatever problem you're facing in a new way. Ask yourself if dealing with that problem is as bad as losing one of your three most important things? The answer is always a resounding NO!

This will give you the push you need to **C**hange your **A**ttitude **N**ow!

Be In the Now

This is another tool that I use in my life to remain on my chosen path and not get flummoxed when the path deviates a little. Being in the now means to quit dwelling in the past and worrying about the future. As an old Buddhist axiom puts it: "Yesterday always is, and tomorrow never comes." We only have today, the present, the now.

One obstacle to being in the now is playing the "What if?" game. Oh, I was a master of *that* one: *What if they don't like me? What if I don't succeed? What if I don't get the job?* Playing this game only stresses you out and kills any possibility of enjoying what already *is*. Can you relate? What have *you* been missing in the now by living in the past or the future?

When I became a teenage single mother, I could easily have given up and been "realistic" about my "bleak" future. Sometimes it's awfully easy to fall into that pit of doom. Because then we don't have to *try* anymore. We can just feel sorry for ourselves and not set goals and not have dreams and live in a perpetual "pity party." You know what I mean.

I decided that was not the life I wanted to lead. I had to switch paths, because my journey was suddenly in an entirely different direction. I had a son I needed to take care of.

I could have beaten myself up with negative self-talk about the "mistake" I had made. I decided it *wasn't* a mistake, that there had to be a *reason* this happened to me. Despite my fear, I decided I was going to live life to the fullest, to live in the now.

I'm not going to pretend that my new journey was easy. It was not. I had some hard times, as I struggled with so many of the things you are probably dealing with right now: trying to balance a career with going back to college, taking care of a family, and, oh yeah, making time for a social life. But I truly believe it is precisely these struggles that can transform us into extraordinary women.

Have you ever had coffee with sprinkles at 6 a.m.? A raspberry white mocha latte with whipped cream piled high, topped with colored sprinkles?

While on the road speaking at a women's conference in Florida, I was particularly tired from a week of traveling and speaking. My feet ached, my legs hurt, and I was *not* going to exercise that morning. I decided to live in the now and treat myself to a special coffee. I had spotted a coffee shop the night before when I was checking into the hotel, and this morning made a beeline for it. I ordered my raspberry white mocha latte...and easily convinced myself that a cinnamon roll with creamy frosting covered in nuts would be a nice addition.

As the coffee lady piled the colored sprinkles on the mile-high whipped cream, my heart sang! Living in the now is truly appreciating the small things, like coffee with sprinkles! I took my coffee and cinnamon roll back to my hotel room, jumped back in bed, and watched Tom and Jerry cartoons until 7 a.m. One of the best mornings I have ever had on the road!

Did I feel guilty? Well, *nope!* Living in the now means we also get to enjoy and spoil ourselves once in a while. We need it and deserve it. So go savor *your* "coffee with sprinkles!"

Change Your Perspective

Changing our perspective is looking at experiences that happen to us in a new way. I learned a life-changing technique at a workshop given by Gail Cohen, author of *How to Reach Your Personal Best*. With Gail's permission, I would like to pass this technique on to you, and I want you to take a few minutes to really do it.

First, think about a time in your life when you had a negative experience, anything that caused you hurt, anger, or embarrassment. Relive it a little, think about it, then write down every negative feeling you experienced. Take two minutes. Ready? Go.

Okay, now let's look at that same experience, but from a different perspective. For the next two minutes, write down all of the *positive* things that came out of that negative experience you just wrote about. Ready? Go.

Before I asked you to write the positive things down, had you ever even thought about that negative experience in *any* positive way? I didn't think so!

I did this exercise in New York City toward the end of a session on stress management. There were many tears, lots of reflection, and a few lightbulbs that turned on for the first time. One very courageous participant, who I'll call Janine, approached me after the conference and, with a tearful smile, asked me to read her evaluation of me as a speaker. She had written: "Yesterday I wanted my life to end. Today I live anew. Thank you, Candy!"

Whew!

Perspective. What an amazing difference it can make in our lives if we simply change it! Do Gail's exercise every time your perspective is stopping you from becoming the person you choose to be. You will be amazed at the results.

What did choosing my attitude, being in the now, and changing perspective do for me? Well, this young princess gave birth to a prince on May 5, 1981. My son and I moved into our first apartment when he was 2 years old; four years later, I bought our first home. He is now a 22-year-old, independent, smart, funny, kind, and loving young man who has taught me so much.

And I picked up another prince along the way—Brad and I have been married for 16 years and have a 15-year-old daughter, Alex. Brad was my rock when I was determined to go back to college so I could become a professional speaker.

When I was 17 years old, I was just a statistic. Now I'm a happy wife, a contented mother, and a professional speaker and author, traveling nationally and internationally, sharing my stories and triumphs!

What is stopping *you* from becoming the person you choose to be? As women, we all have choices, but too many have been jammed into the "could of" or "should of" or "I don't have time to" file cabinets of our lives. Pull them out!

I believe in you. So *you* can believe in you.

Never settle for less than what your heart is calling you to become.

Candy Whirley brings any room to life with her energy, enthusiasm, and dynamic personality. Her stories and activities not only make learning fun, but help participants retain and apply what they have learned. Her main goal is what she calls "edu-tainment," learning while having fun.

She is a frequent speaker on topics ranging from leadership for women and communication skills to customer service, stress management, and creativity for clients as diverse as Hallmark Cards, Cigna Health Care, the Federal Aviation Administration, and the Kauai Fiulipino Chamber of Commerce. Her down-to-Earth style has won over audiences nationally and internationally.

As owner of her own company, SBG Services LLC, Candy not only develops and delivers these training programs, she also volunteers her time working with teenagers and young adults in her community.

Success
of the
Mind

Tara Bazar

CLIMB EVERY MOUNTAIN

There I was, green with fear, wondering if I had made the right decision. I was dangling from a rope more than 200 feet off the ground, telling myself not to look down. Sweltering in the 110-degree Las Vegas heat, my palms were sweating, my arms were shaking, and I was certain I was going to die. Did I make the right decision? Did I really want this? Was this goal really important to me?

Whenever we start to pursue one of those big, gut-wrenching goals, it must be really important to us or we wouldn't think of taking it on. But when that paralyzing fear hits, something inside us screams, *Quit!* And sometimes we find ourselves taking the "chicken exit." Do you know what a chicken exit is? Have you ever been in line for a roller coaster or similar ride and started having second thoughts? You were trapped like cattle, going with the flow, slowly approaching the ride you now feared. When you got to the front of the line, just before you had to step onto that roller coaster, you saw it: an exit sign! At Disneyland that sign says, "This is your last chance to exit."

Well, that's the chicken exit. We carry that exit around with us all the time, and it sounds like this: "Oh, it's not really that important." "I have the rest of my life to do that, so I'll just start later." "I have to wait until the kids graduate from college." "Maybe I can have that when I retire." "Oh, I'll just start that diet on Monday. What's three more days?" CHICKEN EXIT! And when we say these things to ourselves, we buy into them hook, line, and sinker because, in that moment, they are our absolute truth.

We, as women, think too much. Sometimes we think so much that it stops us from acting on our goals or from moving forward. In college, my behavioral psychology teacher would start every class by writing the same quote on the board: "Overanalysis causes paralysis!" We think too much, plan too much, and prepare too much. We dutifully write our goals in our day planners or enter them in our computers. We post sticky notes all around our offices as reminders. We talk about them with friends and family. We get excited and ready for action.

And then, at the very last minute, we let ourselves off the hook. We take the chicken exit. We buy into other people's beliefs. We listen to their fears, doubts, and concerns, then adopt them as our own. We start second-guessing ourselves and our abilities.

Borrowing Fears

As I write this story I am in my 15th week of pregnancy. I just recently started telling people outside my family that I am expecting a baby. And what I have noticed is that other mothers have an inordinate desire to tell me all of their horror stories on the subject. I have enough to worry about on my own; I don't need any help in this area. So, I have to shut that stuff off or it will consume my thinking.

I am a big believer that if something manifests itself in our heads, it will come out in some way, shape, or form in our lives. If it goes on internally, it naturally comes out in our interactions with other people. It expresses itself in our body language, in our facial expressions, and in the words we choose to use. If we want to forge productive relationships with other people and reach those higher levels of success, both personally and professionally, we need to guard what goes on inside our heads.

Changing Your Attitude

According to the book *A New Attitude,* experts estimate that success is 80 percent attitude and 20 percent aptitude. Do you agree that your success has a lot to do with your attitude? I do! I've heard that the average adult has between 40 and 50 thousand thoughts per day…and 87 percent of them are negative! We fill our minds with negativity, we surround ourselves with negativity, and then we wonder why we don't have what we want and deserve! We wonder why we are not accomplishing our goals, why it's so easy to quit.

Some psychological research suggests that we have the ability to change our attitude or our mood in 6.5 seconds or less. That's how fast we can go from a good mood to a bad mood: 6.5 seconds. Have you ever been in a funk for more than 6.5 seconds? Do you know someone who's been in a funk for much longer that that—days, weeks, even years? Amazing, isn't it?

We may not be able to stop the negative messages that seep into our minds, but we can *replace* them as soon as they pop up. There is a three-step process that goes on inside our heads that not only shapes our internal conversations, but also shapes the way we react. This process also determines, without our conscious knowledge, if we "go for it" or if we settle for less than we really want. It's a process that shapes our decision-making ability.

Step 1: The mental aspect

A negative thought or negative self-talk gets the ball rolling on the process. Negative messages include statements such as, *I can't do it, I'm not good enough,* or *I don't deserve it.*

Step 2: The emotional aspect

The emotional aspect comes in the form of a perceived threat, something we make up in our heads. A perceived threat is when we buy into things that are not necessarily true. Have you ever taken just one word that another person has said, examined it, redefined it, and in your head transformed it into some big, huge drama?

Step 3: The physical reaction

For some people, a physical reaction is internal; for others, it's external. Internal reactions are things such as feeling guilty, rehashing a conversation in your head, getting physically sick, shutting down, feeling depressed or lonely, even turning to food as solace. Others have external reactions, which may include screaming and yelling, blaming other people, becoming defensive, storming out of the room, talking about people behind their backs, crying, or rolling their eyes.

It takes all three of these aspects happening within seconds of each other to trigger our negative reaction. These are not things we think about doing. They happen quickly, and if we don't pay attention, they can overtake us and sway our actions.

Changing Negative into Positive

We can't always stop negative messages from entering our minds, but we do have the power to change them, to neutralize them. Ruth Herrman Siress, a wonderful speaker and the author of the *Working Woman's Communication Survival Guide*, says we need to give ourselves a self-talk workout: "Just like you would work out your body, work out your mind."

Here is a sample of her self-talk workout:

Work this out of your system:
   a. I don't have anything worth saying.

Work this in:
   b. I have a right to express my thoughts and be heard.

Work this out of your system:
   a. I am so stupid.

Work this in:
   b. I can learn whatever I need to learn. I am as smart as anyone.

Work this out of your system:

    a. I should be able to get more done in a day.

Work this in:

    b. I have a right to set my priorities and say "no" without feeling guilty.

Work this out of your system:

    a. I look terrible today.

Work this in:

    b. Maybe I'm not a Miss America runner-up today. So what? I'm clean, neat, and smart.

I would like to share my experience in changing negative self-talk and testing the power of my mind, an experience I will never forget.

You Can Cry and Climb at the Same Time

August, Red Rock Canyon, Nevada, 110 degrees. Remember how I was dangling more than 200 feet off the ground at the beginning of my story? Well, that's because I had decided to take my first weekend rock-climbing class. I was ready, or so I thought. I bought all new gear, completely color coordinated, of course. My rock climbing shoes matched my ropes; the ropes matched my harness; and all my carabiners were the same color. I thought that because I looked the part, I would do well. I spent weeks planning, reading, and pumping myself up for the big day.

The first couple of hours of the class were spent going through all of the safety instructions, learning the ropes (literally), and more planning. This was exactly what I needed. I was counting on my team and my instructor, Patrick, and they were counting on me.

I had been climbing indoors for a couple of months and (I thought) had gotten pretty good. I felt I was ready to go. You see, there wasn't a whole lot of risk involved climbing indoors. You could only go so far before you hit the ceiling, and if you fell, you landed on some nice cushy gym mats. So, outdoor climbing seemed to be the next logical step for me. I was pumped!

But as I stood anxiously with the other students listening to the instructor tell us about the climb, I began to doubt my abilities and my existing knowledge. The negative self-talk moved in: *What if I forget what to do? What if I couldn't handle it? What if I fell? What if the rope snapped in half? What if, what if, what if?* Have you ever gotten so caught up in your internal conversation that you missed everything you were supposed to be listening to? Well, that's what happened to me. I wasn't fully there. The next thing I knew, Patrick was asking for a volunteer to go first, and out of nowhere my arm flew up in the air!

Patrick told us the climb I had just volunteered for was about 275 feet.

"I'll climb up to the top, hook up all the safety lines, and when I give you the signal, you start up," he said.

I watched him scale this mountain in about five minutes flat, and I remember thinking how easy it looked. I could do it, no problem.

Patrick gave me the signal and I was on my way. Forty feet off the ground, I was doing pretty well. I had climbed 40 feet in the indoor gym and my body was used to it. One hundred feet off the ground, and I was still moving and still motivated.

Two hundred feet and two hours later, something started to happen to me. My legs started shaking, my arms started shaking, and my mind slipped back into step number one: negative self-talk. I was saying to myself, *Are you crazy? What were you thinking? You'd better get down now. Your legs aren't strong enough, your arms aren't strong enough, and you're not ready to be doing this. You should have listened to everyone else and stuck to climbing indoors. They were right—you don't have what it takes. Just quit, it's not worth it!*

My mind won the fight and I yelled up to Patrick, "Okay, Patrick, I'm done. Let me down." I was trying really hard to take the chicken exit. Patrick had other plans for me.

"You're not done. You haven't made it to the top yet," Patrick calmly told me.

I screamed up to him: "I'm the one paying for this class, so let me down!"

"You can get down one of two ways," he replied. "You can either climb to the top of this mountain and rappel down or you can fall off the mountain."

And then I made that vital mistake, just what everyone had warned me *not* to do: I looked down—and started to panic. I was instantly propelled into step number two: the perceived threat. The chances of me plummeting to the ground were very thin. At most, I might fall a few feet, because I would still be connected to the belay line. Nevertheless, falling off that mountain was not an option. I needed a better plan, and came up with one I thought was brilliant.

My brilliant plan brought me to step number three: physical reaction. I was going to cry, and Patrick would have to feel sorry for me and let me down. I started screaming and yelling. It was very dramatic.

Patrick yelled down to me: "Tara, can you hear me?"

It's working, I thought. I called back up to him that I could hear him.

And he replied, "Good, because you can cry and climb at the same time!"

I obviously needed a Plan B. Plan B was to change the negative self-talk inside my head from, *I can't do it* to *I will get to the top of that mountain so I can* strangle *Patrick.* Sometimes you've just got to tell yourself whatever it takes to overcome those obstacles. I knew that if I kept telling myself I couldn't do it, I never would.

I eventually made it to the top. And as I waited for the rest of my team, I began to realize that what I did to reach the top of that mountain, I could do in so many other areas of my life. Taking the chicken exit, or letting yourself off the hook, is the same as quitting. We would never quit on other people, so why do we quit on ourselves? Why do we place a lesser value on our own success than we do on our children's, for example? Most likely, it is because we get sucked into the three-step process and listen to negative messages.

We all have mountains in our lives that we need to climb. Maybe your mountain is balancing career and family. Maybe it's trying to determine or fulfill your passion or purpose. Whatever *your* mountain is, gear up and climb it. As Oprah Winfrey put it, "Be a queen; own your power and your glory." You can do anything you set your mind to. Believing in yourself and your abilities is more than half the battle.

Preparing to Be Lucky

Not only is it important to give ourselves that self-talk workout, we also have to prepare ourselves to be lucky. Focus on the best-case scenario rather than the worst-case. Accentuate the positive.

Several years ago, a candy company decided to have a contest. They would give $1 million to someone if he or she were able to kick a field goal during halftime at one of the big bowl games. As you can imagine, there were millions of entries into this contest, only one of whom would be given the opportunity to win the $1 million.

One of the entrants began instantly preparing himself to be lucky. He started focusing on the best-case scenario: winning a million bucks. He didn't focus on the bad-news reality, which was that he'd never played a game of football in his entire life!

He didn't know how to kick a field goal or how close to stand to the goal post or how to place the football in the tee. What he did know was that he needed to prepare himself to be lucky. Every day for more than two weeks, he practiced at the local high school, kicking field goal after field goal. And it paid off. During halftime at that big game, his name was pulled. Less than 30 seconds later, he was a millionaire.

Prepare to be lucky!

Commit to the Outcome

The most critical tool in overcoming obstacles—climbing your mountain without quitting—is being committed to the outcome. Without that commitment, nothing else matters.

A young girl by the name of Ashley Cowan wanted to be the first teenager to swim 12 miles across Lake Erie. People tried to talk her out of it because of the danger involved. Her mother told her she would never do it. But Ashley knew the risk involved and was committed to her goal.

Ashley went into intense training for many months. She had the right attitude and the right self-talk, she was prepared to be lucky, and she was committed.

The big day arrived and Ashley was ready. Her coach was going to ride next to her in a canoe, to support her with verbal encouragement (and for safety reasons). Ashley was determined and asked her coach not to let her off the hook, not to let her take the chicken exit. No matter what excuses she came up with, her coach was not to pull her from the water.

Ashley swam strong, but when she was only a half-mile from the finish, fear struck her. She began to quit. She was giving up. She didn't like the nighttime swimming, the dark water, the seaweed, the fish. She was begging, crying, and pleading with her coach to pull her from the water. Ashley had been swimming for nearly 13 hours and was physically exhausted.

Her coach, however, stuck to their agreement. Her coach inspired and motivated Ashley to keep moving and reminded her of her goal and how important it was to her. She refused to pull her out of the water. Gathering strength from her coach and the crowd that was cheering her on from shore, Ashley mustered up her last bit of strength and pushed forward. After 14 hours and 20 minutes, Ashley crossed the finish line. She did not quit.

The most amazing thing about this story is that at the age of 15 months, Ashley was stricken with meningitis and became a quadruple amputee—she swam her heart out for 14 hours and 20 minutes with limbs that were amputated below the knees and elbows.

Despite what some may consider physical limitations, Ashley made it. She did what most people with two arms and two legs would never dream of attempting. At the age of 15, Ashley Cowan became the youngest athlete to complete a 12-mile swim across Lake Erie.

When interviewed after her swim, Ashley was asked why this goal was important to her. She replied, "I just knew if I accomplished this, I could do anything life threw my way." She is a true inspiration.

The evening of my 275-foot climb up that mountain, my body was in excruciating pain. Muscles I didn't even know I had were throbbing. I was in so much pain I could barely walk, let alone climb again the next day. But that evening, I recalled my mother's words to me when I was a child: "If you start something and make a commitment to it, you must always follow through and finish. You can't quit; you have team members counting on you."

Reluctantly, I went back the next day. I couldn't do the climbs physically, but I supported the other people in my group. Because of those words from my mother, I have a strong desire to finish all that I start. It's one of the lessons that has propelled me professionally. It's not always easy; I don't always feel like finishing; I often want to take the chicken exit. But when I feel like quitting, I call my mom for her strong words and the support I can always count on.

Find and cherish your own support person—your mom, a friend, a significant other, a coach, or a crowd cheering you on. We need someone or something that can remind us to replace those negative self-talk messages. If you can't stop the negative thoughts, you can't go any further.

All that you desire is possible—if you don't quit. Don't give up on yourself. And remember, you *can* cry and climb at the same time!

Tara is living proof that it is possible to overcome personal and professional challenges to achieve success. She was once *petrified* to speak in front of an audience, *any* audience. She overcame her fears and now excels as a keynote speaker and seminar leader. Her programs are rich with experiential-learning techniques, interaction, and a healthy dose of humor.

In addition to her work as a speaker and seminar leader, Tara has worked as a counselor in the prison system and helped sexual-abuse victims overcome their trauma. She credits these experiences with helping her to realize that "people are people," and it is always possible to make a profound difference in the lives she touches.

Tara specializes in delivering programs and keynotes that address up-to-the-minute workplace issues, and she is adept at weaving real-life examples and experiences into her presentations. Her clients include SUNY-Albany, the Girl Scouts of the USA, Coldwell Banker, Century 21, the NYS Department of Public Service and Division of the Budget, and Sandia National Laboratories.

Tara may be reached at *www.tarabazar.com.*

Dr. Chérie Carter-Scott

ARE YOU A NEGAHOLIC?

"It won't work!"
"It can't be done!"
"It'll never happen!"

These are the all-too-familiar words of a "Negaholic," a word I coined nearly two decades ago to describe a very common condition—the addiction to negativity and self-doubt that afflicts so many of us to one degree or another.

Negaholism does not discriminate. Negaholics come in all sizes, colors, nationalities, and genders. We can find them in every corner of our world—at home, in church, at the store, in the office. Of course, I have never come across a Negaholic baby—this behavior is learned from the environment, the family culture, and the media.

Where does Negaholism start? How is it fostered? What can we do to change it? For many years, I wrestled with these questions. I wanted to find out why people are so negative and why it is so difficult to be positive.

Our environment is clearly one culprit—we live in a Negaholic world. Have you ever noticed how deliberately TV, the news media, and magazines focus on the negative rather than the positive? They justify this by claiming that conflict is more interesting than harmony. Situation comedies show families putting each other down, using sarcasm, and "one-ups-man-ship" as their normal way of relating to each other. Serial murderers get their faces plastered on magazine covers;

model citizens go uncelebrated. The kids who killed at Columbine and other schools are immortalized; straight-A students and star athletes are relegated to the background.

There are several reasons for the all-pervasiveness of the Negaholic reality. First of all, it is accepted. People expect it, anticipate it, and consider negativity normal. Second, it is reinforced and rewarded. TV talk-show hosts show by example how to belittle people as they put down their guests in front of millions of viewers. Politicians running for public office show us how to discredit and disqualify opponents by attacking their character, past blunders, or personal traits over which they have no control. Bullies learn how to solve their problems by watching their heroes in the movies do so with a gun.

Is it so surprising, then, that Negaholism permeates our individual psyches, making us feel negative, powerless, diminished, and ready to resort to violence to solve our disputes?

When negativity spreads throughout the environment—workplace or domicile—morale plummets, motivation vanishes, productivity slows, and everyone is infected with the Negaholic virus!

The average person, of course, doesn't see herself as a Negaholic. In fact, she thinks of herself as realistic and normal. She sees her perfectionistic tendencies as desired traits that lead to excellence. He sees his feelings of "never measuring up" as motivation to make him strive to be the best. Parents, in turn, transmit these traits to their children, who early on learn that nothing is ever good enough: Their Cs should be Bs, their Bs should be As. And when they do achieve straight-As, it is taken for granted and summarily ignored.

Most people have some trace of the Negaholic virus, not inherently dangerous unless it has become pervasive. Take the following quiz. While not definitive, it will help you assess how pervasive Negaholism already is in your life. Then I'll help you deal with it.

Are You a Negaholic?

1. Do you sometimes have difficulty getting out of bed in the morning? Yes No

2. Do you sometimes focus on the times you "blew it" and things didn't work out? Yes No

3. Do you often find yourself expecting the worst so as not to be disappointed? Yes No

4. Do you sometimes observe yourself feeling anxious when you hear good news, in anticipation of the bad that will surely follow? Yes No

5. When asked, "What do you want?" do you frequently answer "I don't know"? Yes No

6. Do you often hear yourself saying, "It doesn't matter," when you are asked what you want? Yes No

7. Do you often find yourself citing the mistakes, blunders, mishaps, and boo-boos in your past as justification for avoiding another risk? Yes No

8. When imagining a "big goal," do you hear the voices in your head saying, "You can't do that" or "You'll never be able to..."? Yes No

9. Do you have difficulty being enthusiastic about your "to-do" list? Yes No

10. Do you frequently find fault with little things you do? Yes No

11. Do you hear yourself putting yourself down for what you wear, how you walk, what you say? Yes No

12. Do you have lists of things you have never accomplished that you use against yourself? Yes No

13. Do you have difficulty celebrating your accomplishments? Yes No

14. When you start to imagine your goals, do you hear, "Who do you think you are?" in your head? Yes No

15. When you receive a compliment, do you brush it off, dismiss it, or look for an ulterior motive? Yes No

16. When you look in the mirror, do you often count the gray hairs and wrinkles? Yes No

Do you think you could ever...

17. Have the dream home you want? Yes No
18. Have the ideal relationship that you want? Yes No
19. Make the amount of money that you want? Yes No
20. Have the body you want? Yes No
21. Have a satisfying, rewarding, enjoyable job? Yes No

Do you frequently get angry at yourself...

22. For spending too much or being a cheapskate? Yes No
23. For eating too much? Yes No
24. For drinking too much? Yes No
25. For wasting time? Yes No

Do you frequently feel...

26. Angry at yourself or others? Yes No
27. Anxious (in general or for a specific reason)? Yes No
28. Confused about what to do? Yes No
29. Depressed about anything or nothing? Yes No
30. Hesitant? Yes No
31. Impatient? Yes No

32. Insecure?	Yes	No
33. Lonely?	Yes	No
34. Regretful?	Yes	No
35. Unhappy?	Yes	No
36. Unloved?	Yes	No
37. Worried?	Yes	No

Do you seldom feel...

38. Calm?	Yes	No
39. Capable?	Yes	No
40. Certain?	Yes	No
41. Competent?	Yes	No
42. Confident?	Yes	No
43. Enthusiastic?	Yes	No
44. Happy?	Yes	No
45. Joyful?	Yes	No
46. Lovable?	Yes	No
47. Optimistic?	Yes	No
48. Powerful?	Yes	No
49. Satisfied?	Yes	No
50. Do you constantly work and strive but rarely experience completion and satisfaction?	Yes	No

Figure Your Score

In order to determine the degree to which you are addicted to Negaholism, here's how to score yourself on this quiz:

- Give yourself 2 points for every YES answer to questions 1-15.
- Give yourself 2 points for every NO answer to questions 16-21.
- Give yourself 2 points for every YES answer to questions 22-37.
- Give yourself 2 points for every YES answer to questions 38-49.
- And if you answered YES to #50, give yourself another 2 points.

If your score is:

0   Congratulate yourself for having a positive self-image, high self-esteem, and being well on your way to a healthy, full life.

1-24   You have a mild case of Negaholism, but you have very little to worry about. With some affirmations, positive reinforcement, and pats on the back from yourself and loved ones, you will do just fine.

25-40   Negaholism probably runs in your family. If addressed now, you could nip it in the bud. Left unattended, it could grow into something extremely detrimental to your mental health. A consciousness-raising group, self-esteem workshop, therapy, or self-help group(s) would be advised. Also read one positive-image book per quarter to get yourself on the right track.

41-60   You need to take your condition seriously. Without proper care and attention, you will become a certified Negaholic. You need some form of positive input each week to turn this condition around. A chart on the wall with stickers and stars, journal-writing, listening to self-help or positive-image audiotapes in your car or before going to bed, one self-help book per month, and 10 daily written acknowledgments will help cure this advanced condition.

61-80   You are in the danger zone. No longer can you cover up, take things in stride, or hope it will all clear up when you lose the weight, get the job, land the relationship, or move to the right place. Face facts: you are seriously addicted, and you need to come to terms with it. There *is* hope—you are not a lost cause. But you must take the first step: acknowledge that you are a Negaholic and affirm that you will do what it takes to arrest this addiction.

81-100 You are a confirmed Negaholic. You need to admit it and take immediate, daily steps to arrest this addiction. It has grown to be bigger than you—the negativity is so subtle that you hardly even notice it; but it pervades your thoughts and feelings. You need an external program to detoxify yourself from the negative demon within. Read this book and take action! Start immediately. A new life is waiting for you now—a positive self-image is in your future.

If the quiz revealed some traces of Negaholism in your life, don't panic. It is not the end of the world. It's more like noticing that first gray hair—now that you've seen it, you can do something about it!

In order to change any habit, pattern, or behavior, it takes six steps. That's it! If you follow the six steps faithfully, you can overcome any unwanted behavior. Look closely at what the quiz says about you, then decide what you want to change. When does that unwanted behavior occur? What time of day? What people do you tend to be around when the behavior is present? What is in your control to change?

The 6 Steps

1. The first step is to become aware of it. That was the purpose of the Negaholic quiz—to heighten your **awareness** of any personal negativity.

2. After you are aware, you can then **acknowledge** what you noticed—accept it as true.

3. The third step is the most important: You must **choose to change**. This is the most powerful step. Say to yourself, *I don't want this anymore, and I want it to be different.*

4. After the choice has been made, you must create a **plan** of how to shift from where you are right now to where you want to be.

5. Any plan will encounter successes and setbacks along the road, but **monitoring** your progress is essential to get you where you want to go. Monitoring means checking to see if you are on track or not—you count cigarettes, pounds, or strokes off your golf game. If you never monitor your plan, it becomes simply an intention—something you want but don't necessarily achieve. Monitoring your plan lets you build in corrections when you have fallen off the horse and to validate, recognize, and reward your successes. Monitoring can be the longest step in the process, but it is the difference between making a New Year's resolution and keeping it long enough to achieve the results you want.

6. **Celebration** is the final step in the process. You must remember to celebrate your successes. Once we have climbed the mountain, we tend to absorb and incorporate all new and breakthrough experiences in our reality.

If you follow the steps outlined here, you can transform any Negaholic tendency into happy, healthy, and productive behaviors. You have the power to make all your dreams come true. May you manifest all your heart's desires and become the person you've always dreamed of.

New York Times best-selling author Chérie Carter-Scott, Ph.D., has been coaching and empowering positive changes successfully since 1974. Dr. Carter-Scott is an author, entrepreneur, consultant, lecturer, teacher/trainer, talk-show host, and seminar leader. Her company, Motivation Management Service Institute, Inc. (MMS), has reached millions of people worldwide. Some of her Fortune 500 corporate clients include AMI, FMC, American Express, IBM, GTE, State Farm Insurance, AMI, SGI, Burger King, and Better Homes and Gardens magazine.

Her New York Times best-seller, If Life is a Game, These are the Rules: The Ten Rules for Being Human, has been published in 34 countries and is used as a textbook at more than 100 colleges and universities throughout the country. Other books in this series include If Love is a Game, These are the Rules; If Success is a Game, These are the Rules; and If High School is a Game, Here's How to Break the Rules: A Cutting Edge Guide to Becoming Yourself.

Dr. Carter-Scott has promoted her books across the world, including appearances on a wide variety of TV programs and networks, including The Oprah Winfrey Show, Leeza, CNN, Ananda Lewis, Iyanla, The Other Half, Montel, Sally Jesse Raphael, Politically Incorrect, The Today Show and more than 400 other television and radio talk shows.

Other published work includes Negaholics: How To Overcome Negativity and Turn Your Life Around, which has sold more than 100,000 copies; The Corporate Negaholic: How to Successfully Deal with Negative Employees, Managers and Corporations;

and two self-published books, *The New Species: The Evolution of the Human Being* and *The Inner View: A Woman's Daily Journal.*

She lives in Nevada and Santa Barbara with her husband. Her Websites are: *www.themms.com* and *www.drcherie.com.*

Dr. Courtney Anderson

ENTREPRENEURSHIP

So you want to be an entrepreneur? Own a business? Be your own boss? Finally have the freedom to do as you please when you want to? No more boring office, crazy coworkers, and demanding supervisor who doesn't respect you.

You are certainly not alone. Why are so many get-rich-quick schemes and work-at-home scams based on the dream of breaking out of the 9-to-5 world and taking control of our financial and career choices? Because they know that's what we want!

I watch late-night infomercials that promise if I simply buy their product or service, I can be as happy and rich as the "regular" people they trot out as endorsers. After all, they, too, were losers just a few short months ago. These beaming people now have a life most of us can only dream about (we are assured), and, as the infomercial promises, *I can too,* because if they could do it, I can do it. There is even a no-risk, money-back guarantee. How could you lose?

I want to assure you that the freedom these schemes, scams, and ads promise *is* available, *is* real, and you *can* have it. But it won't come in the mail or from a television ad. The freedom to do *what* you want, *when* you want, and to make as much money as you want while doing it, *can* be your reality. But it requires hard work. It requires sacrifice. And it is very, *very* high-risk.

I know, because I am one of those people who has attained this freedom. The purpose of this chapter is to share with you some of what I have learned up to this point.

I have had the pleasure of spending my entire adult working life pursuing, and ultimately realizing, the entrepreneurial dream. Whenever people ask me what I do, I always respond that I don't have a job. I retired from backstabbing coworkers, long hours, low pay, and demanding bosses when I was 25.

I have had the opportunity to take on different challenges and to experience different aspects of my intellectual, creative, and professional interests. I have spent time as a university professor, a professional singer, a corporate trainer/consultant with my firm LitigationMitigation.com, an attorney, a writer, a real estate investor, and a motivational speaker. But I have not had a day of "work" in quite a few years, and I do not intend to have one in the future. I enjoy large parts of every day and consistently have the peace of mind that I so desperately craved while an employee.

I don't want to paint too rosy a picture: I do love *every* day, but my life is not a blissful, trouble-free fantasy. I sincerely doubt that anyone who has walked the Earth has had a perfect life. Yet the stress and the gnawing discomfort that I experienced as an employee have dissipated and been replaced by an eagerness and an anticipation that makes every morning feel like Christmas Day when I was an 8-year-old child.

If this sounds a bit too good to be true or reminds you of a bad infomercial, I apologize. I do not intend to offer a clichéd, tired message stating that if you only believe, then anything is possible. I consider myself to be a rather pragmatic person; some would even call me cynical. I certainly do not have the personality type to regurgitate platitudes and call it a day. I have come to this point in my life, a committed believer in the power of entrepreneurship, simply by witnessing the tranquillity it brings to my life.

How Did I Ever Get Here?

I wake up most days excited to discover what is going to happen. I dream about what deals are going to go through and what new, once-in-a-lifetime opportunities will present themselves. I have been able to do some awesome things. Sometimes, when I hear myself telling someone else to take control of their attitude and that they can achieve anything that they aspire to, I am shocked that the words are coming out of *my* mouth. The irony that I now positively motivate and inspire other people is not lost on me; I spent many years as an angry person. In fact, I was such an angry, sullen, depressed person that I was reprimanded and booted off both my junior high and high school cheerleading squads for my low "pep" and lack of "cheer."

I grew up in a highly stressful military household. By the time I finished high school, I had moved at least eight times and lived everywhere from my birthplace in Germany to rural Yakima, Washington; urban Fairfax County, Northern Virginia; Leavenworth, Kansas; and in Kentucky and Texas. I did not grow up in a home of satisfied parents, and I was a shy person who was always the new kid in school. I did not develop trusting relationships with many other individuals. Due to the large geographical distance from my extended family, I was never really able to develop close ties with my relatives, seeing them only in the summer and on holidays. Even all these years later as an adult, I envy the close bonds between my cousins who grew up together and continue to have lifelong emotional support and friendships.

I have always had a problem with authority figures (a key characteristic of many of the other entrepreneurs I know). As a young child, I did everything I could to be invisible in school. As I got older, I just didn't bother going very often. I was bored in most of my classes and never fit into the socializing politics of cliques and popularity. I always felt like an outsider and sought refuge in books, art, music, and ideas.

I have always been comfortable expressing my opinions and didn't refrain from doing so in school, which was not appreciated by most of the teachers and staff. I never thought of my actions as being disrespectful, but I certainly felt that my inability to conform to the expected norms made me a target. I cleverly deduced this from the copious amounts of detention time I was awarded.

I never thought I would live long enough to achieve and enjoy life the way I do now. I used to fear that I would never find love in my life. I actually told myself that I was both unlovable and incapable of loving anyone. I loathed myself and engaged in behavior that was so self-destructive that I almost killed myself. I intentionally subjected other people to my own deep, emotional pain and bitter disappointment.

I am convinced my childhood made me an entrepreneur, with its requirement for self-sufficiency and my own inborn rebellion against authority.

So How Can You Do It?

Money is not needed to succeed as an entrepreneur, nor connections, education or special skills, or gifts. I know that I—a young, black woman—have been able to amass assets beyond my wildest dreams with little initial capital, no connections, and scant help from anyone else.

To succeed as an entrepreneur, two characteristics are vitally necessary: an unyielding, overwhelming confidence in yourself and your abilities; and the near-maniacal willingness to be utterly obsessed, committed, and passionate about the possibilities that others will insist are totally impossible. In spite of their opposition, you must see, feel, touch, and taste your goals, such that you will not give up, even in the face of failure.

And you *will* fail. Catastrophically, monumentally, embarrassingly, and shamefully. But if you are imbued with the entrepreneurial spirit or gene (I am not certain, but I do believe that you either have it or you don't), you shall not be deterred by failure, by ridicule, or by the agony of defeat.

What else do you need? What else are you up against? Here's what I think I've figured out:

Tenacity

This is the stubborn refusal to give up that many business texts proclaim is the core value of a successful entrepreneur. Is it? Well, if it isn't, it is certainly in the top three! The best way to develop the tenacity you need to succeed (presuming it is not an indelible part of your nature) is to identify situations in which you refused to quit and made it to your goal. Personally, I find the experiences in life that are most inspirational, that I can rely on for that shot of mental adrenaline when I'm down or tiring, are not the successes I've had as an adult. Rather, I learned some of my most important lessons early in life, and those are the experiences I use to bolster myself when I'm feeling overwhelmed. Remembering these successes rekindles our desire to tackle new challenges and make ourselves proud of what we can do—if we want to badly enough.

Self-respect

If you lack self-respect, you will fail as an entrepreneur (and probably in many other areas of your life, as well). At some point, you will need to convince others to work with you, give you money, and believe in you. How can you expect them to storm the ramparts for you, if you yourself don't believe in your abilities? If you don't value yourself (and by extension your ideas, dreams, and opinions), you will fall off the entrepreneurial path very, very early in the process. And there really is no substitute—all of the education, money, or prestigious titles in the world will not make up for low self-esteem.

A touch of madness

Many well-intentioned people will call you "crazy," "nuts," or worse. In fact, if you *haven't* had anyone refer to you as "that crazy s.o.b." (or worse), you're doing something wrong! Several people who truly *care* about you must tell you, directly and repeatedly, that you are totally out of your mind to do_____. Only then should you feel confident that you are on the right path, because only then will you have left the comfort zone where most people live. The line between madness and genius is minute, and you will cross it.

Obsession

This is tenacity to the nth degree. If you are truly meant to be an entrepreneur, you *will* be obsessed about your dream, business, or invention...and called obsessive by your friends, family, and other loved ones. It is par for the course and to be expected. You will probably neglect activities and relationships that are important to you as you maniacally strive towards the success that you can see, feel, hear, taste, and touch so clearly that it fills your every waking hour.

Others will *not* be able to see what you see; they will call you delusional. Do not despair. When you succeed, these same people will state that they believed in you all along and never doubted your eventual success. Be gracious and do not contradict their memories. What is important is that you remember and cherish what you accomplished, despite their criticism and disbelief.

Loneliness

Get comfortable with this word—it will be a key description of your existence in the early years of your pursuit (if not forever). Your zealousness will be an individual experience, one almost impossible to share with another person unless she is equally obsessed. And the responsibility you will feel, not just for your own well-being, but for the lives of your employees, is one that cannot be shared or ignored.

Self-discipline

When you are on your own, no one else cares if your work gets done, or you have any customers, or, for that matter, if you even get out of bed in the morning. Oddly enough, although "Courtney Employee" would never have won an attendance award, "Courtney Entrepreneur" is amazingly focused on my own businesses. If you need to depend on someone else to motivate you, direct you, help you when you fail, and pat you on the back when you succeed, do not become an entrepreneur!

Humility

Nothing is more displeasing to potential clients, customers, or business associates than someone who is condescending, patronizing, or stuck up. Do not take any of your success for granted, because you will experience catastrophic failure—all entrepreneurs do at some point. Remain humble and you might get some help when you stumble, rather than a round of hearty applause.

Inner peace

This should be the goal of all of your hard work. You should be striving to quell the uncomfortable feelings associated with having to ask for permission to do something from an authority figure. As an entrepreneur, you get to schedule your own breaks, hours, and benefits, and you don't have to beg permission from anyone.

"No"

This is the magic word that leads to inner peace. You will say it often to other people to ensure that you are in control of your business, and that your business is not in control of you. Saying and acting on this magic word will allow you to reclaim the most precious asset you own—your time.

"Yes"

This is the magic word you will use often with yourself. The most important employee you have is yourself. Thus, when you need a vacation, you will say yes. You will not deny yourself relaxation, time off, healthcare, romance, and fun. You will not answer your mobile phone, e-mail, phone, or fax when you are not "working." You will not miss important life events (weddings, funerals, graduations, baby showers, etc.) because you are too busy working. You will say yes and attend these events to ensure that you have a *life*. Work is not a life. It is *work*.

Likewise, there are two things that are, in my humble opinion, guaranteed to doom your chances of making it on your own:

1. Listening to others. At least until you have a modestly successful business, don't consider the opinion or input of others. Entrepreneurs have the special gift of *not* listening to other people. This is what allows them to create businesses, ideas, and items that never existed before. If you let them, people will tell you that you are taking too much of a risk, that you need to have a back-up plan, that your idea really isn't that good. They will also be happy to tell you why they are so sure you will fail—you lack money, experience, talent, or connections, or you're too old, too young, too ugly, too dumb, too smart...you get the idea.

Ignore these people. Remember that when they speak, they are simply exposing their own fears about themselves. Do not indulge them in their attempts to turn you into a defeated pessimist.

2. Laziness. I have to be blunt: This presents the biggest challenge for most people, but it is one that must be overcome. Along with all of the positive characteristics we have already discussed, there is one that is undeniably required: a devotion to hard work. In your early years, you will be alone. If you don't do it, no one will.

You're Ready to Go. Now What?

The first step to take is to define what type of life you desire. The saddest statement I have ever heard was from a very close friend of mine several years ago. We were discussing her career plans. "What are your dreams?" I asked her. "I don't have any," she replied. And it was clear she had convinced herself that was the truth.

Once you honestly determine who you are and what you desire, you may (have to) admit to yourself that you don't *want* the responsibility of establishing, running, and growing a business. You may prefer a work environment where you are part of a team, or seek a great supervisor who offers the leadership, mentoring, and support you need.

That's fine. The high-risk, high-stress lifestyle of an entrepreneur is only for those of us who *just don't fit* anywhere else, for those who crave freedom and autonomy more than stability and safety.

But those of you who *do* hear the siren call of the road less traveled and are *not* satisfied to be someone else's employee, heed the call!

Your Most Valuable Business Skill

I have learned that the most important tool for financial, social, physical, and mental success is to ask questions. If you do not understand something, ASK! I have found that what separates fulfilled, joyful individuals from sullen, miserable complainers is often the fear of asking. You will never know what could be, if you do not seek and try new things, new ways, and new experiences.

I don't know everything; in fact, I don't know everything about any one thing. I have faced extreme failures (business failures, bankruptcy, abusive relationships, and being fired from 26 jobs), yet I live a life today of true beauty. I have the freedom, the love, the adventure, and the financial stability that I craved. I owe it to my now-ingrained habit of always asking for more out of this precious life.

Your Most Valuable Business Asset

Time. You cannot get it back, and you don't how much you have left. Isn't it ironic that so many of us are taught the purpose of living only through another's death? I know that I have grown most from the losses I have faced, because they continually remind me that this is all temporary, that I am breathing on borrowed time. I have drastically turned my life around at different junctures, and I received much of the strength to do so from the deaths of those I have loved.

I dedicate this chapter and owe my purpose in life to the most extraordinary women I have ever had the privilege of knowing and loving: my aunt, Marjorie Pryor; and my grandmother, Edythe Heslip.

I have not learned, although I am knowledgeable.
I am not experienced, although I have experienced life.
I am brutally aware of the transitory nature of everything around me, yet I
am obsessed with creating permanence.

Life teaches, if we remain always open to learning.

A creative, dynamic, and nationally renowned motivational speaker, Dr. Courtney Elizabeth Anderson, JD, MBA, is also an attorney, author, educator, entertainer, and entrepreneur. She currently focuses primarily on her training and consulting firm, Litigation Mitigation, specializing in all areas of leadership, personal empowerment, and employment law workplace compliance (with more than 100 engagements a year). Her unique approach—integrating leadership skills with knowledge of the law—has motivated, inspired, enlightened, and transformed the way organizations manage to minimize their legal liability.

As an attorney, Dr. Anderson is in private practice as a solo practitioner in Austin, Texas, primarily practicing Entertainment Law, with selected Business Law and Criminal Defense casework.

As an educator, Ms. Anderson has served in primary, secondary, and university institutions (both public and private). She has served on the faculties of the University of Texas at Austin and Huston-Tillotson College, teaching business law, and is currently an adjunct professor in the MBA program of Ashington University, teaching strategic marketing and operations management.

As an entertainer (singer, songwriter, producer, choreographer, director, and radio talk show host), Ms. Anderson has garnered acclaim with her introspective and unique art. Her new album is slated for release in early 2004.

An author of both fiction and nonfiction, she is already at work on her next nonfiction work set for release in early 2004, *Passing for Sane: Creating Contentment out of Chaos.* She currently resides in Austin, Texas, with her miniature dachshund, Marley Anderson.

Dr. Anderson can be reached through her Website, *www.CourtneyElizabethAnderson.com,* or toll-free at 1-888-899-0692.

JoAnn Corley

THE HONOR OF WORK

"It takes courage to grow up to be who you really are."

—*e. e. cummings*

The sun shone brightly through my office window as I prepared to meet with a new career-coaching client. Several years earlier after experiencing my own transition—filled with soul-wrenching evaluation and an ongoing confusion as to what to do with my work life—I started my coaching practice. That evaluation has led me to this day.

I heard a knock on the door and peered through the door's window. There, appearing sheepish and uncertain, was Jennifer. She had been referred to me a week earlier by a friend. I could tell from her demeanor that this would be an interesting first meeting.

I was to learn later that, like her parents, Jennifer had been a scientist most of her adult life and had reached a somewhat prestigious level in her profession. She had recently been "mutually separated" from her employer, a well-known candy manufacturer.

I invited Jennifer in, offered her tea, and suggested she begin by telling me her story. As the next hour unfolded, I listened intently as she told me about her childhood; the controlling, assuming relationship she had with her mother; and the absent involvement of her father.

She explained how both of her parents were scientists and how it had been expected that she would become one, too. It had never been a question of what *she* wanted, but what was expected. Certainly, it was most important to continue the family legacy. Jennifer's parents even accompanied her to college to help her pick out her classes.

As Jennifer, now in her mid-40s, described in great detail her formative years and the factors that had influenced her career path, her countenance started to change. Her eyes lifted, a smile emerged, and her body shifted. I believed an epiphany was coming on!

A new sense of energy appeared as Jennifer began to recount points in her career where messages from the universe, as she put it, were telling her that being a scientist was not for her. As she delved deeper into her work performance, she began to see how she had been subtly sabotaging herself. She clearly realized that, deep down, she did not want to be a scientist and was rebelling against her parents' control and the lack of initiative she had taken in her own career choices.

She revealed to me that she was really an artist at heart, had loved playing the trumpet, and had even considered being a teacher. In the weeks that followed our first meeting, we began to explore the issues that had prevented Jennifer from taking control of her life early on and why it had taken so long to get to this point of significant recognition. In my view, she was finally growing up!

As we worked together, there were several stages I took Jennifer through to maximize her epiphany and to transform it into a realistic transition plan.

Stage 1: Taking Responsibility

Taking responsibility in any part of a growth journey is essential. I found this to be one of the hardest steps for Jennifer, who had to wrestle with the continuous blame she directed at her parents. That blame kept her from accepting the fact that she did not claim her adulthood and chose to stay a child in the context of her relationship with her parents. They didn't want to let go, and she didn't challenge them.

This cycle of blame kept Jennifer disempowered and trapped, a victim to her upbringing. She began to recognize that if she continued to participate in that cycle, she would never be free to connect with her personal power. (Personal power is our ability to be ourselves, fully and authentically.) Jennifer would need that power to recognize, honor, and express her true self to her parents and prepare herself to move forward.

She learned that one of the ways to express personal power is through decision-making—a significant indicator that reflects whether she was expressing what she wanted or what someone else wanted. In her life experience to date, at least in the area of her career, she had been expressing her parents' wants and desires, not her own.

Once Jennifer was able to clearly identify the points along the way at which she had not taken adult responsibility, she was able to connect with her personal power and move to the next step.

Stage 2: Forgiveness

In order to continue to connect and nurture her newfound personal power, Jennifer and I had to work through the next stage, which was forgiving all involved parties—her parents *and* herself.

First, we established a clear distinction between accepting blame and accepting responsibility—the former nurtures self-pity; the latter, self-learning.

Next, we talked about the need for Jennifer to forgive herself. She had to accept the fact that it was her responsibility to separate from her parents, and given the circumstances, she had done the best she could have at that time, even though it had led her to the unpleasant place in which she now was.

Forgiveness brings on a powerful release. Jennifer began to experience this as she embraced its healing powers. The experience, she said, was the vehicle she used to ride out of her past and into her present. And there she stood, a woman in her mid-40s, finally ready to live an authentic present, fully capable of crafting an exciting future—this time of her own design!

Stage 3: Comprehensive Assessment

The next step I took Jennifer through was a thorough assessment of her skills, likes, dislikes, values, hobbies, talents, life experiences, motivators, childhood dreams, personality type, and work style. We compiled all that information into what I call a Personal Portfolio.

At this point in Jennifer's journey, it was important for her to see her true self, identifying as many dimensions of herself as she could. Because she had ignored much of who she was for so long, she had to be resurrected and nurtured, acknowledged and honored.

This was an interesting stage for Jennifer. In addition to discovering and uncovering, Jennifer had to begin to accept the "self" that was emerging, both her strengths and her limitations.

Though Jennifer had received clues all along her journey that being a scientist was not for her, her self-worth was deeply tied to her self-image as a successful scientist.

That presented a challenging dilemma. She had to struggle with the question of what her life would be worth if she *wasn't* a scientist. In her world, what you did determined your worth, not who you were! Making that distinction was critical for Jennifer's successful journey through this process. Her career did *not* define her value as a person!

Combined with establishing this distinction, there was a brief period when she struggled with seeing and accepting her whole self. It really didn't match how she saw herself or how her parents saw her. In order for her to keep moving forward, she had to be successful in this stage as well, even if the new image was met with disdain by her parents.

New realizations emerged as Jennifer examined the details of her work life. She recognized that she had limits in terms of the amount of work she could handle at any one time, and that the things she was genuinely interested in would perhaps lead her to careers that would not generate as much income as she was used to.

She also began to question the role she wanted work to play in her life. She discovered that she didn't want it to be as dominant as in the past. She was now beginning to consider work as something that gave her the financial means to help her develop other interests. This was a huge value shift for her. She came to the decision that she didn't really want to spend much of her personal energy on a career, but wanted to use it to pursue resurrected interests.

As part of the transition, I encouraged Jennifer to begin to pursue many of the things she loved but had abandoned in her earlier years. She began playing the trumpet for fun and cooking her favorite recipes. She even joined her church choir. Her heart and spirit were expanding, and she was gaining a healthy balance in her life.

At the heart of this stage, Jennifer began to redefine her whole view of work: what it meant to her, the role it would play in her life, and how it would serve her, rather than her serving it.

Paradigms emerged. What ended up being the turning point for Jennifer was her newfound understanding that *any* work is honorable if one approaches it with integrity. No matter how much or little someone earns, all work is honorable, all work serves the human community, and all work has value. Of course, her most significant transition was understanding that work did not define her value, but that she gave value in the work.

Armed with these newly adopted values, Jennifer was able to move freely and effectively into and through the final stage of her transition journey.

Stage 4: Realistic Action Plan

Finally, Jennifer and I were able to move into the stage of constructing a realistic action plan defining how she was going to proceed with the next part of her work-life journey. This plan included determining what parts of her past work experience and key qualities she wanted to use in her future employment. She would also need to educate herself on the market for each of the options she wanted to consider and how she would match that reality to the new dreams she was formulating.

It was so exciting to participate in her journey. It was like watching a tightly tucked rose slowly unfold and blossom. There was an energy and glow about her that was so attractive and contagious.

As Jennifer identified career possibilities, one of the options that appeared on her list was none other than teaching—a prior dream. One day, as she was scouring the employment ads, she came across an ad for a part-time chemistry teacher at a local college. She could potentially use her experience to teach college-level science—that hadn't occurred to her before!

Jennifer was beside herself at our next meeting, and with great enthusiasm talked through the need to test this career direction. She decided to apply. A week later, I received a call from Jennifer, who proudly announced she was employed as a chemistry teacher.

Jennifer was now taking to heart two of my favorite sayings that I had shared with her: "Action brings clarity" and "Action attracts opportunity." In the days and weeks that followed, Jennifer proved both of these to be true.

Several weeks after beginning her new job, it was clear that she loved it. Jennifer discovered that her early dream of being a teacher was really representative of her true heart. She loved the interaction with the students and the deep sense of impact she was having—even teaching chemistry!

Your work is the most important work you'll ever do! Only YOU can do it—uniquely you!

We take our careers for granted—in most cases, we don't even plan our work lives. Instead, we use what I call "pin-ball" career planning: bouncing from job to job whenever someone pulls the lever. In fact, many of us will spend more time planning our retirements than we will ever spend planning our work lives.

Each of us is a unique human being with a particular work purpose. As we become fully ourselves, doing the work we were meant to do, we experience a rich life, which spills out into service for the human community. No matter what job you hold, from janitor to judge, if done authentically and with integrity, it is honorable.

The work you were meant to do is yours for the taking. Please do not live someone else's life—live only yours, fully and completely.

As Helen Keller once said, "I am only one; but still I am one. I cannot do everything, but still I can do something. I will not refuse to do the something I can do."

The choice is yours. I hope you dance!

JoAnn Corley is a dynamic, insightful and passionate speaker, trainer, and personal development coach. She travels throughout the country speaking on diverse topics that address tapping and cultivating human potential. It is her mission to inspire, teach, and lead people to have meaningful, quality lives.

JoAnn uses her 20-plus years of business experience and thousands of hours of human behavior counseling to consult in areas ranging from organizational and management development to career planning and small-business startups.

She founded Convergence Consulting Group, a human resource/organizational development firm, in 1998. It provides consulting services to major companies in a wide variety of industries and professions, from accounting and engineering to staffing and sales. Her coaching clients have ranged from scientists and engineers to mid-level managers and small business owners.

JoAnn currently resides in a western suburb of Chicago, IL. She may be reached at *www.unlockthepotential.com*.

Jan Fraser

DEALING WITH DIFFICULT PEOPLE

I find it amazing that while I, of course, am perfect and always a joy to be with, so many other people are so darned difficult to work and live with. What is wrong with them?

We've all met them—the Know-It-Alls, the Stabbers, the Bullies, the Whiners, and those other types who drive us to distraction. And let's be honest—maybe *we* have oh-so-occasionally lapsed into some of the difficult behaviors I'm going to describe in this chapter. Yes, it's true, we're *not* always perfect.

But it is essential that we learn to identify the particular behaviors that each type represents, analyze our own responses to them, and learn how to deal with each one. First and foremost, it's imperative that we maintain a sense of humor when dealing with the difficult people in our lives. Though that may at first seem impossible, it is critical. Otherwise, we will internalize the stress their challenging behavior inevitably causes. And as I'm sure all of you can attest, we don't need more stress in our lives!

So, lighten up! Yes, it can be scary, even intimidating, to have to live or work with some of these types, but the tips that I'll share with you in this chapter will help you keep that humor equilibrium and not be at the mercy of these folks.

Here they are, in all their challenging glory.

The Know-It-All

She clearly knows more than anyone else on the planet, and with no prompting at all is prepared to expound in excruciating detail about anything...and everything...forever.

Okay, let her! Once you know you are dealing with a certified Know-It-All, ask her for more information on whatever she's talking about. When she reaches the end of her monologue, ask her to tell you more. Whenever she seems finished, ask her again to tell you more. At some point, she will *finally* come to the end of what she supposedly knows about that subject.

At that point, you are ready to say some magic words, hopefully with a bit of a smile: "It's comforting to see that, like the rest of us, your knowledge on any given subject is limited. Welcome to our world."

It may take a few doses of this technique to take root, especially with extreme Know-It-Alls. But just keep repeating it. She needs to hear it and you need to say it if you are ever to survive her!

The Talker

He has talked non-stop his entire life and plans to spend the winter at your desk telling you every detail of everything that's ever happened to him. Unlike the Know-It-All, he is not necessarily erudite on any subject. He'll just talk about anything! Forget the fact that work is piling up on your desk and his—he is oblivious to everything except his need to tell you his story.

Wait for him to take a breath, then jump in with "I would love to hear more about this, but I have to get a report out by noon," or, "I am in a time crunch today and just can't give you the full attention this obviously deserves." If the story is actually work-related, you could say something like, "That sounds like something the marketing department would want to know about. Why don't you forward your idea to them?"

I have resorted to asking my own Talker friend, "Will this be a two-, five- or 10-minute conversation?" When she acts surprised (and she always seems to), I tell her that I want to give her the full attention she deserves and need to know if we'll have enough time to do justice to her story.

If you faithfully follow these suggestions and your verbose friend, spouse, or coworker still plagues you daily, buy a roll of yellow "Caution Tape" at your local home improvement store. When you see a Talker heading for your office for an hour-long discussion on the woes of their day, stretch "Caution Tape" around your desk or, to really make a point, right across your doorway. It may not stop them from entering, but they will have to be particularly thick-headed not to get the message!

The Gossip

The Gossip uses every opportunity to create mayhem in the office (or life) by passing along stories—true or, better yet, not—about others. It makes them feel powerful to be able to get people to listen to them. And the juicier the story, the more people will be intrigued.

When a Gossip starts to tell you a story about a friend or coworker, gently interrupt her and say, "Gee, she (or he) never says anything bad about you," and walk away. If you aren't sure if it qualifies as gossip, just ask yourself, *Is it true? Is it kind? Is it important?* If your answer to at least two of the three is "no," why listen to this person? Move on.

Gossip is taking over the businesses of America. If we all refuse to listen, the Gossips will finally get the message. As Mother Teresa said, "Kind words can be short and easy to speak, but their echoes are truly endless."

The Hysteric

Hysterics missed their calling—they should have majored in drama. An Hysteric believes everything is a crisis. There is simply no such thing as a mole hill in an Hysteric's atlas, just mountains. And they *love* to get everyone else as worked up about everything as they are.

An Hysteric can keep the office on a giant roller coaster, which is why it is important to avoid buying into their behavior. Simply nod your head and, every minute or so, say, "I understand." This comment does not mean you are agreeing with them, it just means you are acknowledging their message. If an Hysteric asks you a question, respond with short replies—a simple yes or no works great! What they crave most is an audience, so do not let yourself be drawn into their self-styled drama. Be warned: Your utter calmness in the face of their unending drama may make them more hysterical!

The Beauty Queen

Eleanor Roosevelt once said, "Remember, no one can make you feel inferior without your consent." Beauty Queens would try even Eleanor's patience.

The Beauty Queen spends more time on her hair and nails than she does on any project at work—she is primping, plumping, and pruning herself all day long. She frowns on others who (she thinks) are not as beautiful as she is and is always ready with a barbed comment about anyone who isn't up to her superficial standards.

To resist the temptation to tell her where to stick her nail file, you need to have developed your own self-esteem affirmation, along the lines of *I am loving myself each and every day in every way; I am celebrating my beauty both inside and out; or I am fully listening and acting upon my inner beauty.* When this person invades your space with her obnoxious messages about what *you* should be doing to beautify yourself, just repeat one of your affirmations silently to yourself until she finds some other poor soul to pick on.

When a Beauty Queen cattily asks why you don't fix your hair a certain way or go on a diet or change that awful outfit, stay calm. Do not let her embarrass you, especially if she has an audience. Responding angrily or acting hurt will only mark you as a steady victim.

Instead, say to her, "I'm confused. Why would you mention that to me at this time?" Now the ball is back in her court, and she has to justify her inappropriate comment. Just remember to stay calm, repeat your internal affirmations, and never let her judgments affect the serenity of your soul.

The Pleaser

The Pleaser wants to please everyone, every day, in every way. I know how easy it is for women to fall into this category because I did for many years. I was taught to be seen and not heard. So I didn't speak up or voice my opinions, and I always went along with what everyone else wanted to do.

The problem with a Pleaser is you never know what he wants to do or where he stands on any issue. And his mousy acquiescing to you and everyone else can really be irritating...sometimes you just want to shake him until he actually gives an opinion. Of course, Pleasers don't think they're irritating. As far as they are concerned, they are just about the most accommodating folks around. What's wrong with not forcing your opinions on everyone else?

What happens, of course, is that you try to get their opinion, they don't give it to you, and then they resent the decision you make because it doesn't agree with their (unexpressed) choice. Eventually, the grudges build up and, when you least expect it, the Pleaser explodes like the time bomb he is.

The next time a Pleaser refuses to express an opinion, tell him that his view matters to you and you *do* want to know what he really wants or thinks. Keep encouraging, even forcing him to speak up for himself.

The Stabber

The Stabber will try to hurt you, either openly—right to your face—or secretly—behind your back. They want you to know they have power and you don't, or they want to take away whatever power you do have.

A Stabber needs to be dealt with aggressively—ignoring her behavior will not make her go away or lessen her resolve. A back-stabber, for example, can be confronted with, "I understand someone is speaking about me behind my back; I need you to let them know it must stop today or I will take further action."

A person who openly sabotages your work also needs to be directly confronted. I ran into this situation when I was working at the ticket counter of a major airline. During a period of downsizing, I was given the choice of leaving or being reassigned as a ramp agent, which was a nice way of saying I had to load bags on the aircraft. It was the most difficult job I have ever had. I was lost in a man's world and not feeling very sure I could complete my daily tasks. It took all my stamina and courage to return every morning. My legs became wilted carrot sticks each day as I lifted more than I ever thought I could.

All the other men were helpful, except for the Stabber, who happened to be my supervisor. He tried to intimidate me every day, making me lift things most of the men couldn't have handled—heavy boxes of fish packed in ice or aircraft tires that had to be wheeled up the ramp into the cargo hold. Every day when I walked into the break room, he'd stop talking with his friends and just stare at me. I knew he had been talking about me. I was miserable and had to do something. My self-esteem was suffering.

I stewed and stewed about my situation and finally came up with a great solution. I walked up to him the next morning and said, "We both want the same things in life." He looked startled and asked me what I meant. "*You* want me off the ramp," I smiled, "and I want to *be* off the ramp!" He nearly smiled as he realized I was right. "But if you continue to sabotage my work," I continued, "they'll never move me...and I'll be in your face in the break room till we both turn gray."

He thought that over very carefully and said, "I see what you mean!"

From that day forward, my Stabber and I had an understanding. It was a win-win solution for both of us. Within a few weeks, based on good reports from my now-supportive ramp supervisor, I was transferred back upstairs to the ticket counter.

The Whiner

The Whiner has a negative comment about everything that happens and most everything he sees. He has probably gotten away with complaining for most of his life because no one had the guts to shake him out of his comfort zone. He is not fully mature—whining got him what he wanted in childhood and it seems to be working for him still.

Ask him how he would remedy whatever situation he's complaining about. Ask him for his suggestions for fixing the problem. If he has none, then he is not entitled to complain. You'll need to let him know that every time he raises an objection: "I tried to involve you in the process, but you gave me no input. I need you to get behind the decision that was made without complaint."

The Bully

Bullies win by intimidation, using anger, negativity, and even violence to get what they want. One woman told me her boss throws a stapler at her...once a day. That man definitely qualifies as a Bully!

Bullies are great at reading your expressions and reactions and gauging your vulnerability. If your body language is passive and your facial expression weak, they know they have you in the palm of their hand.

Most Bullies are actually frightened people with low self-esteem, so be ready to stand up to them. Look them right in the eye, even if you are a mass of nerves inside. Stand your ground. You have rights.

But don't put yourself in harm's way. If they threaten violence or become violent, don't try to be a heroine—call security. And question whether you want to work at a company that would tolerate such behavior.

Where Do We Fit In?

I hope these brief descriptions and prescriptions have shed some light on some of the people you have to work or live with. But let's not be too ready to blame everyone else—all these "types'"—for the problems we confront each day. These pat descriptions are all well and good, but we have a little of each type in us, don't we? Even if we aren't too ready to admit it? And perhaps there are times when *we* are the ones everybody else is having trouble with. Rarely do we see ourselves as others see us.

So let's start by admitting that a great first step to better communication is to identify and confront our own failings. Let's stand outside ourselves and view from a distance our interactions with others. We are always ready to make judgments about what others should or shouldn't do; perhaps it is our reacting to what they are doing that causes us pain.

Ask a nurturing friend about the last time *you* were difficult to get along with. Why do they think you acted or reacted as you did? And what can *you* do to be less difficult in the future. If this person is truly a good friend, listen to his or her message with open honesty.

What if we looked upon others as different, not difficult? Do you think that would change how we viewed our daily interactions? I believe it would.

Let's look at the difficult people in our lives from different angles. Let's strive to free ourselves from the hurtful reactions caused by others. Let's work to know ourselves with greater clarity and strive to gain greater balance and joy in lives.

Most important, let's make sure the most difficult person we have to confront each day isn't ourselves.

Jan Fraser is the very definition of a "self-starter." During her early career in the airline industry, she rose from the ramp support team to the ticket counter to flight attendant to *instructor* of 20,000 flight attendants. At Delta Airlines, she earned the "Feather in Your Cap" award for going above and beyond service requirements, and she received the "Professional Flight Attendant" award—for outstanding attention to customers' needs—while at American Airlines.

Jan later became a member of American's Performance Solution team, speaking on self-esteem, life balance, stress reduction, and exceptional customer service throughout the United States, as well as in South Korea, Japan, Guam, Australia, Turkey, Italy, and India.

Since leaving the airline industry, Jan has conducted training for a wide variety of Fortune 500 companies, prisons, library systems, associations, and schools, including General Electric, Home Depot, Verizon, Bell Atlantic, Medtronic, the U.S. Air Force and many others.

Jan founded WomensConferences.org to offer support to the struggles and life-balance issues facing so many women today. She is the creator and author of Women's Success Journal, an original bimonthly e-zine.

Her personable style, sparkling humor, and "extra-mile" attitude have made her a popular keynoter and seminar leader. She may be reached toll-free at 1-866-BookJan, or via e-mail at jan@womensconferences.org.

Claudia A. James

In "Let Your Light Shine" on page 215, I share my most recent challenge—a broken ankle. In comparison to another period in my life, this inconvenience is "a walk in the park."

About a decade ago, every night for two years, I ended my day with a mother's plea, asking God to protect my children, begging Him not to take them from me, to keep me safe and at their side until they were self-sufficient and emotionally healed. Then, after a minute or so of silence, I would wipe my eyes, let out a long sigh, and continue praying: "Lord, I'm ready to come home—the emotional pain is unbearable." A double-sided prayer? What a paradox! Yet how symbolic of a woman facing the world alone.

On March 8, 1990, my parents' 48th wedding anniversary, my mother passed away in her sleep. My beautiful, spirited mother had put up a good fight, but her body was a lemon and it had finally been recalled. Following my mother's death, Dad moved in with us. It was a natural transition—he was in poor health, and I was the only one of their six children who survived infancy. It quickly became apparent that his skills, honed during 30 years in the military, could best be utilized in the plush retirement center near our home. On the day of his move, as we backed out of the driveway, he looked back at our lovely home and said, in a sad reflective voice, "Can I come back if I don't like this place?" Those words pierced my heart. As his only child, I believed I had let him down.

A few months later, I learned I was losing my college instructorship—the campus where I was teaching was being eliminated. Being low on the tenure pole, I, too, was being eliminated. When I walked out of my classroom for the last time in February 1991, I began another grief process. What the heck was next? Three weeks later, on the day my husband and I had planned to attend our daughter's district music competition and play golf, the children and I were thrown into an abyss that would take years to climb out of.

It was a beautiful spring morning when I awoke to the smell of freshly brewed coffee. Upon entering the kitchen, I saw my husband sitting at the table; he looked as if he, too, were just waking up. His cup of still-steaming coffee was sitting in front of him, and his head was resting in the palm of his hand. It took me almost a minute to realize his transition had come quickly and quietly. The father of my children, the man I had been married to for 23 years, and with whom I thought I would spend eternity, was gone—an explosive heart took his life so fast we didn't get to say good-bye.

Shortly after my husband's funeral, my father had a stroke and I had to admit him to a nursing home. He died soon after. Leaving my dad's room for the last time, I headed down the corridor to the exit. With each step, my breathing became more labored and my body felt as if it were in a plaster cast that was getting heavier and heavier. Attempting to keep grief from consuming me, I leaned against the corridor wall and began breathing deeply. The feeling of aloneness engulfed every part of me. Whatever awaited me beyond the doors of the nursing home, I realized, I would now face by myself.

The night looked different, the stars and moon were not illuminating the sky—the overcast was not only in the sky but in my heart as well. As I drove away with tears streaming down my face, I took another deep breath and thanked God for the years I had with them—my mother, my father, and my husband—and then, from the core of my being, I asked God for the strength to face the world alone.

At 42, I found myself orphaned with no siblings, widowed, unemployed, and the single parent of two teenagers to get through high school and college. My first concern was to secure my estate, so if something were to happen to me, the children could maintain their lifestyle. Next, I contemplated my career options, and after major soul searching, I decided to start my own speaking/consulting practice, to dedicate the remainder of my life to helping women secure their futures.

You never know when tragedy will strike and how quickly you will have to be responsible for every aspect of your financial life. The Cinderella story is only a myth. Even if you are lucky enough to meet a real-life Prince Charming, statistics show you will probably outlive him by an average of eight years. Presuming you make it that far—47 percent of all marriages end in divorce.

The median income of unmarried women over 65 years of age is $11,161 per year.

Take the time and make the effort to educate yourself about your current financial situation and to become more involved in where your assets are and what your money is doing. Following are the tools you need to organize your finances, to invest your hard-earned money, deal with credit and credit cards, protect your assets, and cut costs, when necessary.

Tools for Organizing Your Finances

Tool #1: Rent a safety deposit box

◆ Contents: personal property appraisals; bills of sales; original birth certificates/death certificates/marriage licenses; government papers; passports; visas; military papers; naturalization papers; securities; CDs; deeds; powers of attorney; wills; trusts; car titles; video of personal property including contents of home, cars, and so on.

◆ When establishing a safety deposit box at your local bank, consider adding at least one more name—someone you trust. If you only want them to access it in the event of your death, sign a

POD (Payment on Death). If you only want them to access it if you are incapacitated, give them a power of attorney.

Tool #2: Purchase a fireproof box

◆ Contents: copy of billfold contents; income tax returns (going back seven years); appraisals and certificates of authenticity of art/collectibles/antiques; jewelry/clothing appraisals; property tax receipts; insurance policies; warranties.

Tool #3: Copy important papers to an attorney (or friend/relative)

◆ Contents: burial instructions, including: service outline, bio, and obituary; names and addresses of person(s) given power of attorney; copies of wills; power of attorney trusts; living will; healthcare directives.

Tool #4: PODs/TODs and powers of attorney

◆ POD (Payment on Death)/TOD (Transfer on Death) authorizations give your beneficiaries quick access to your assets. I recommend them for certain assets.

◆ A durable power of attorney, given to someone you trust, will protect your assets in the event you become incapacitated; it may even contain a healthcare proxy.

Tool #5: Calculate your net worth

◆ List all your assets (what you own), whether paid for or not.

◆ List all your liabilities (what you owe). Do not list things you can cancel, such as utilities and insurance premiums.

◆ Subtract your liabilities from your assets. The difference is your net worth.

Tool #6: Assess your spending

◆ For the next month, keep a log of everything you buy—do not judge your acquisitions, just record them.

◆ Draw a line through the ones that do not relate to your goals.

◆ Create a budget using the items you did not cross out.

Tool #7: Create a budget

◆ To adhere to your budget, try to see it as "planned spending" rather than "restrictive spending."

◆ Designate 10 percent of your gross earnings for retirement income/emergency money.

◆ Designate a small, weekly or monthly stipend you can spend (without guilt) on anything you want.

◆ Make certain it reflects your values—what you believe is important.

Tool #8: Create a financial notebook

Include sections such as:

◆ Legal papers and where they can be found.

◆ Financial plans: three-, five-, and seven-year plans, including strategies.

◆ Loans/credit cards. List account number, financial institutions, and current principal balance due for each.

◆ Net worth statement (balance sheet) and budget.

◆ Names and addresses of key people (pastor, attorney, CPA, bankers, doctors, etc.).

◆ Insurance coverage: Name of company, type of policy, coverage amount, agent's name.

◆ POD/TOD authorizations—Power of attorney and Payment on Death authorizations.

Tools for Investing in the Market

Tool #1: Create a financial portfolio

A financial portfolio is like an artist's portfolio—each contains a collection of items expressing the creator's individuality. The financial portfolio contains a collection of cash/cash equivalent instruments, stocks, and bonds.

◆ **Cash/cash equivalent instruments.** The standard recommendation for an emergency fund is three- to-six-months' income. These monies need to be in financial instruments that can be easily accessed, such as savings accounts, short-term CDs/T-bills, and money market accounts. These instruments are usually low-risk and low-interest bearing.

◆ **Stocks (equity securities).** Stocks are designed for growth—the younger you are, the greater the possibility your portfolio will contain mostly stocks. While stocks often provide the highest return, they are also the highest risk. If the organization doesn't make a profit, neither do you—if it folds, so do you. Why? Because you are a part owner.

◆ **Bonds (debt securities).** Bonds are designed for income—the older you are, the greater the possibility your portfolio will contain mostly bonds. The return on bonds is oftentimes less than that of stocks, but they are less risky because you are a creditor, not an owner.

Tool #2: Invest in companies that match your interest/values

To increase the odds that you will roll with the "ebb and flow" of the market, be prepared to "stay the course" for at least seven years. And to increase the odds that you will not pull out in a down market, invest in organizations that share your same values and interests.

Tool #3: Invest when it is right for you

Regardless of what some financial planners may tell you, there is no right or wrong time to invest in the market—it is all based on your situation. The general rule of thumb is to buy low and sell high. Considering the average cost per share (dollar cost averaging) may be more effective than waiting for a stock to hit its all-time low before buying it...presuming you can figure out just when that is!

Tool #4: Join an investment club

Get active in an investment club and/or join the National Association of Investors Corp. There are a number of calculations you will learn, including the Rule of 72, which tells you how long it will take you to double your investment at different rates of return.

Tool #5: Know what to expect from Social Security

An Earnings and Benefit Estimate Statement is provided by the Social Security Administration (SSA) on at least an annual basis. When you receive this information, verify all the reported earnings. If there is a mistake, call the SSA immediately to get it corrected so it doesn't impact your retirement benefit. As you plan for your retirement needs, the SSA recommends that your Social Security Benefits represent only about 40 percent of your total retirement funding, providing you are an average earner. (Studies have shown that you will need 70–80 percent of what you are currently earning in order to maintain a similar lifestyle in retirement.)

Tools for Handling Credit and Credit Cards

Tool #1: Credit reports/reporting bureaus

At least every two years and/or whenever there has been a major change in your credit history, secure a copy of your credit report from each of the three major credit reporting agencies. Check these reports for accuracy. Your ability to get credit is based on these reports and the credit score they contain.

Tool #2: The Fair Debt Collections Practices Act and The Fair Credit Billing Act

Know your rights. Both of these federal acts and the related state statues can be accessed on the Internet. When your rights have been violated, report it to your state Attorney General's office.

Tool #3: Credit cards, charge cards, ATM cards/debit cards

When debt is used to create a positive outcome—student loans, home mortgages, etc.—it is considered good debt. When debt is used for instant gratification—an unplanned shopping spree—it is considered bad debt.

- ◆ Use a charge card rather than a credit card—you are required to pay the bill each month with a charge card.

- ◆ Avoid using a credit card or a charge card for non-emergency purposes unless you can write a check for the acquisition at the time of purchase.

- ◆ Don't use your credit cards for purchases of less than $25 or for those not included in your spending plan.

- ◆ Keep your cards current by using them at least every six to 12 months; otherwise, the company may close your account. (A little available credit is good.)

- ◆ Write "ID required" on the back of your cards rather than signing them—this will eliminate any unauthorized use.

- ◆ Using an ATM/debit card is more risky than a credit card—because you are fully responsible for any unauthorized usage.

- ◆ On at least one day per year, use cash for all your purchases. James Stowers of American Century has instituted October 16th as National Cut-Up-Your-Credit Card Day.

Tool #4: Limit the amount of credit

A good rule of thumb is not to have more than 30 to 40 percent of your gross earnings committed to monthly payments. This amount includes any credit you've cosigned for.

Tools to Protect Your Assets

Tool #1: Health insurance

A good health insurance policy is comprehensive, including both basic protection and major medical. If you are carrying an individual policy, shop around and compare prices. To keep the premium cost affordable, consider a higher deductible. If you are married, and both of you are carrying full coverage through your employer's group health policy and paying for at least part of the coverage, re-evaluate the benefits of being doubly insured. A tie-in plan may be less expensive and still cover all your medical costs.

Tool #2: Disability insurance

If you're providing the main source of income for your family, how are your assets protected if you become disabled? Review your company's policy on sick leave and disability insurance. Consider enrolling in your company's disability plan or taking out a private disability policy.

Tool #3: Life insurance

- Life insurance may be necessary if you want to do any of the following: financially protect your family members, make financial resources available to your creditors, and/or leave a lump sum (beyond your net worth) to your family or a favorite charity.
- There are three basic types of life insurance: whole life, universal life, and term life. Whole life and universal life policies have a built-in savings factor called *cash value*. I recommend them for supplementing your retirement. Term insurance has no cash value, but is great for short-term protection during your younger years. I recommend it to cover your indebtedness.

Tool #4: Long-term care insurance

This type of insurance pays for nursing home care, intermediate care, custodial care, home healthcare, and respite care. According to the American Association of Retired Persons (AARP), women represent 75 percent of all nursing home residents, the average cost ranges from $50 to $200 per day, and the average stay is 30 months.

Tool #5: Homeowner's insurance

Review your policy at least once a year. Is there adequate coverage for jewelry, furs, antiques, and collectibles? Is your home office insured? Would your home or personal property be replaced at today's value? Is the personal liability coverage large enough? The higher your net worth, the more coverage you may need. If you are a renter, consider renter's insurance to cover your personal property.

Tool #6: Auto insurance

Liability coverage is the most important part of your coverage because it covers bodily harm to another person or their property. Generally, $300,000 per accident is recommended, or twice the value of your net worth (according to AARP). Depending on the age of your vehicle and/or your reserve funds, you may only want to carry liability insurance, rather than incurring the cost of full coverage.

Tools to Cut Costs

Tool #1: Avoiding impulse buying

◆ When their energy level is low, people have a tendency to buy too quickly, often compromising the quality, price, and/or style. If your energy level is low, go home and reenergize, perhaps by working out.

◆ When their self-esteem is low, people have a tendency to "overshop," buying not just a new suit, but the accessories, too. If your self-esteem is low, go home and create a values clarification list, articulating what is important to you.

◆ When their checkbook is low, people have a tendency to use credit cards; consequently, they usually pay more for an item than if they paid cash for it. If your checkbook is low, go home and clean out a closet. I bet you'll find something you forgot you had.

Tool #2: Gift-giving

◆ Either limit the amount you spend on your friends' gifts or give them a gift of your precious time.

◆ Limit your gift-giving to family members, perhaps just to the youngest members of the family.

◆ Limit the amount you spend: Does your child really need $150 tennis shoes?

Tool #3: Cutting small costs

◆ Start by cutting small costs: daily lattes, unread newspaper/ magazine subscriptions.

◆ Turn off QVC and avoid watching commercials.

◆ Switch to private label grocery items. They often contain the same ingredients as the name brands, at significant savings.

Tool #4: Eating out

◆ If you dine out a lot, resolve to eat at least one or two more meals a week at home.

◆ Avoid drive-thru restaurants. Prepare your own convenience items when you have time and store them in the freezer. Carry them with you on day trips and skip the fast food.

◆ Use coupons.

Tool #5: Buying in bulk

Unlike 20 years ago, buying in bulk is now more of a convenience than a method of savings, and you are paying for that convenience. Before buying the Giganto size of anything, compare the per unit (pounds, feet, ounces, etc.) price—then make your purchase if you are truly saving money.

Tool #6: Grooming

◆ Minimize the amount of times you wear make up—perhaps only when you're in public.

◆ Simplify the products you use. Get rid of any items you haven't used in the last 12 months.

◆ Buy your foundations at the department store cosmetic counter and your mascaras/eyebrow pencils at the drug store.

◆ Frequent a beauty college rather than a hair salon.

◆ Buy a new accessory rather than a new outfit.

◆ Create an "Exchange Clothes Day" with friends.

Tool #7: Transportation

◆ Save on gas consumption by running all your errands on one day. Create an errand map so you're not driving duplicate miles.

◆ Save on auto insurance by driving older cars, but be certain you maintain them.

◆ Consider buying a used car rather than a new car—let someone else take the first year's depreciation hit.

◆ Use an auto consultant when making a car purchase. For a reasonable fee, they will find the car you want and negotiate the price—all you have to do is sign the paperwork and pick up the car.

Tool #8: Utility studies/audits

Utilize a consultant to evaluate your utility costs, particularly your phone bills. For a small fee, they can often save you plenty of money.

◆ ◆ ◆

All of the preceding tools are just some of those I've used over the years to accumulate and protect my estate. When I need a nudge in using some of these tools (or others) I think of what's called the Baby Philosophy: "If something stinks, change it."

It's been 13 years since I began re-creating myself. The children are grown and gone now, and so is the overpowering feeling of aloneness.

Today, I give thanks for that period in my life, because I gained a deeper intellectual, spiritual, and emotional perspective that aids me in helping other women secure their futures.

Claudia has presented more than 700 workshops throughout the world on topics ranging from finance, customer service, and team development to interpersonal communication skills, career mapping, and spirituality. A top trainer, speaker, and author, she brings more than 30 years of combined corporate, teaching and volunteer experience to her many endeavors.

A successful owner of James Educational Meetings and Seminars (JEMS), which she founded in 1992, Claudia is a great speaker, a gifted storyteller, and an energetic leader. She is often seen and heard on a wide variety of local radio and TV talk shows. A *cum laude* graduate of Missouri Western State College, she is an adjunct faculty member at several area colleges, an original mentor in the Women's Network for Entrepreneurial Training, and a member of various local and national professional, civic, and women's organizations.

Claudia's ability to make a complex and intimidating subject like finance is a credit to her 15 years' corporate financial experience. She has presented keynotes on the topic as well as been a facilitator and speaker for Women's Financial Information Programs (WIFP), a governmental initiative for women of all walks of life presented nationally in collaboration with AARP.

Claudia may be reached at 1001 NE 86th St., Kansas City, MO 64155. Phone: 816-420-8686; e-mail: jemscaj@aol.com.

Judi Moreo

ATTITUDE IS A CHOICE

Themba was a beautiful, well-educated African girl, daughter of a dignitary, tall and proud…with a bit of a chip on her shoulder. She was attending one of our six-week training programs at the office in Johannesburg where she worked. We had spoken of the effects of attitude on our lives many times, and she felt justified in having a defiant one. We had often asked her, "Is your attitude getting you the results you want in your life?" And she had admitted it was not.

Even though she worked in the city, she lived in a township and rode a taxi to work every morning. Taxis in South Africa are minivans that usually carry twice the number of passengers they were designed for.

One morning, Themba was late for her training class. When she finally arrived, she was visibly shaken. I was so concerned by her appearance that I stopped the class and asked her what was wrong.

"When I tried to get into a taxi this morning," she replied, "the taxi driver said to me, 'Not you. You don't get in my taxi. I don't like your face.' Well, you know me. Normally, I would have fought with him. But I decided I would listen to your lessons about attitude. I just stepped back and waited for the next taxi. Another lady took that seat.

"Another taxi arrived almost immediately and I got in. About two miles down the freeway, we watched as that other taxi had a blowout on the front tire and rolled over. Everyone in that taxi was killed.

"I don't mean to buy your face (*translation: I'm not trying to impress you*), but this morning I heard your words again and I heeded them and they saved my life."

"What words were those, Themba?"

"You said that sometimes it pays to lose a battle in order to win the war, and choosing the right attitude determines a better outcome. If I hadn't kept my attitude in check this morning—if I had insisted on getting in that taxi as I normally would have—I would be dead. Your words saved my life. Thank you."

Attitude *Is* That Important!

Now this is a pretty dramatic example, but it certainly demonstrates that the attitude we choose every day causes either positive or negative experiences to manifest in our lives.

Time and again, we hear that having a positive attitude is the key to all success in life.

Well, it is!

The exciting thing, if only we would realize it, is that our attitude is one of the few things in life over which we have complete control. We *can* close our mind to failures, negative people, and past circumstances. We *can* discipline our minds to take possession of our thoughts.

American psychologist William James once said, "As you think, so shall you be." These words have always resonated in my mind, and I work daily to discipline my mind to maintain a positive focus. When I allow my mind to be filled with fear and doubt, that's when I scare away any chance of the success that I want so badly.

So What Is Attitude?

You may be asking yourself, "What has attitude got to do with taking control of my success? And what is this thing called attitude anyway?"

Some people will argue that it is something you were born with. Others will say it is brought about by the circumstances of life. I don't believe either is true.

Our attitude is the outer expression of our inner feelings. Our thoughts create our feelings, and our feelings determine our behaviors. So when we improve our thoughts, we improve our feelings, which improves our behavior, and leads directly to improved results.

It is important to process our thoughts so that they move us forward in life, not hold us back. If we remain positively focused on what we want in our lives, we won't have time to get sidetracked by things and circumstances we don't want.

Why is it for many of us that when a difficult experience comes our way, we interpret it as a hardship? A child doesn't think that way. When a little girl is learning to walk, she falls down...and gets up again. It's not a problem. She doesn't analyze it. She doesn't say, "If I don't get it right this time, I'll give up." She just *does* it and doesn't worry if she's walking straight or crooked, toes in or toes out. She just concentrates on where she wants to go.

And so should we!

When things happen to us, we can *choose* to believe they happened for the best. We can discover opportunities in the most difficult experiences *if* we are willing to look for them. It is what we *think* about each experience that determines how we respond to it. If we think, "This is a disaster!" it certainly will be. On the other hand, if we think, "There's an opportunity in here somewhere" and look for it, we will most certainly find it.

5 Steps to Changing Your Attitude

Step 1: Learn more

Acquire as much knowledge as possible about whatever it is that you would like to be, to do, or to have. The more you know, the more confident you will feel. Confident thinking leads to a positive attitude, which leads to success.

Step 2: Identify the pitfalls

This second step may seem a bit negative at first, but do it anyway: Identify what could go wrong with your plans. If you know the pitfalls, it's easier to work around them. Unknown factors breed fear. Once you expose fears to the light of day, evaluate them, and start exploring ways to overcome them, they will no longer seem so scary.

We naturally experience fear whenever we step out of our comfort zones. Think back to your first day of school, when you started a new job, or took a trip by yourself. You were a little afraid, weren't you? But once you stepped out of your comfort zone and did it, it wasn't so bad after all. You could do it!

Examine your fears. What is making you hesitate? Do you feel you lack skills? Money? Education? Have you done your homework? Do you know how much skill, money, or education you really need? Or is this supposed lack just a convenient excuse?

You CAN do whatever it is you want to do. You just have to sell YOU on doing it.

Step 3: Learn positive self-talk

Self-talk is the conversation you have with yourself. Your self-talk is what creates your self-image, your level of self-esteem, self-confidence, and your attitude.

Our minds have such power. The subconscious part of our minds doesn't know the difference between real and imagined, so it will say yes to whatever we tell it. If we tell it we are intelligent, confident, and strong, it will say, "Yes you are!" and direct us down the path to success. Of course, if we tell it we are dumb, weak, and scared, it will also say "Yes" and take us on the road to nowhere.

Equally important is what we ask ourselves. Stephen Covey, writing in *Executive Excellence*, suggests we ask the question: "Am I going to live my life to be governed by daily activities in accordance with noble principles?" In other words, am I just reacting to life, or am I living my life in a proactive manner? Am I so busy putting out fires that I don't have time to start any? Am I allowing my life to be governed by outside forces, or am I choosing to live my life in accordance with my own decisions? Do I have important goals and dreams that I'm committed to, or am I creatively avoiding commitments by filling my life with activities?

Step 4: Make daily affirmations

Repeat to yourself constantly: *I have the ability to achieve my goals.* Keep repeating it. It won't be long until you will believe it. This is called an affirmation.

To affirm is to state that something is true and to maintain that it is true in the face of any and all evidence to the contrary. Repeating an affirmation leads your mind to a state of consciousness where it accepts that which it is told.

In his book, *The Magic of Believing*, Claude Bristol tells us, "This subtle force of repeated suggestion overcomes our reason. It acts directly on our emotions and our feelings, and finally penetrates to the very depths of our subconscious minds. It's the repeated suggestion that makes you believe."

So begin each day with an affirmation. Repeat to yourself: *I am intelligent. I am effective. I am happy. I am healthy. I have the power to achieve my goals.* Or whatever else you would like to believe about yourself. Keep your sentences short, which will make them easy to remember.

How often should you do your affirmations? In addition to every morning, I recommend doing them:

- ◆ At the end of each day, before going to bed.
- ◆ Any time you hear a negative statement from yourself or from others.
- ◆ Any time you have doubts about achieving what you want in life.

Once something is recorded in the subconscious, it will stay there, replaying itself until you choose to displace it and diligently work to do so. Every statement you make to yourself has an effect on your subconscious. So be careful what you say to yourself!

Step 5: Surround yourself with positive people

Close your mind to other people's negativity. Negativity is a virus, and it *is* catching! Make yourself immune to it by understanding that no one else can make you angry. No one else can make you sad. No one else can hurt your feelings. Unless you allow them to! You *choose* how you react and respond to situations and what others say and do. They can trigger old feelings from the past, but they cannot determine how you feel or how you behave. How you react or respond to what they do or say is up to you! Learn what your hot buttons are, examine why they set you off, change your thinking about the situation, and you can control your behavior.

Okay, that's the five-step plan. If this all sounds like a lot of hooey, try it for yourself. Don't discuss it with anyone else until after you have tried it for a minimum of 21 days and know it works. Many people will try to convince you that you shouldn't try it. They will tell you that it's ridiculous, that it won't work.

Don't believe them! Try it.

Maintaining Your New Positive Attitude

Even the most successful people have experienced periods when they have been confused, disillusioned, and discouraged. Yet they have overcome these trials and tribulations to achieve triumph and victory because they have chosen the right attitude. When we feel discouraged and stressed; when life seems intolerable, even meaningless; when our lives are not going the way we want them to; and when events are taking place so fast that we don't know the questions, never mind the answers, doesn't it make sense that we should take control of our thoughts, so that we, too, can triumph?

Life comes to us in a series of challenges, and the attitude with which we choose to perceive these challenges and the mindset with which we prepare for them determines whether our lives are rewarding or not.

Victor Frankl, a Jewish psychiatrist who spent World War II in the same concentration camp where his wife and child were killed and the manuscript that was his life's work was destroyed, later wrote a book titled *Man's Search for Meaning*. In it, Frankl asked himself why some people gave up and died under the difficult circumstances of a concentration camp while others not only survived, but grew stronger. From his observations, he concluded that the answer to this difficult question was attitude: "What made the difference," he wrote, "was how people chose to perceive the experience." In any given set of circumstances, he decided, "everything can be taken from a person except the ability to choose one's attitude."

By now, I hope I've convinced you that we *do* choose our attitude. And once we've made the choice, we owe it to ourselves to maintain it.

Following are the techniques that I use.

Goal-setting

Goals give us a purpose in life: They give us a reason to get up in the morning, a reason to go to work, and a reason to come home at night. What do you want out of life? What do you want *in* your life? Where do you want to go? What do you want to be? To have? To do?

Write everything down, then visualize each goal. Having a clear picture in our minds of exactly what we want—seeing the details, the colors, the complete picture—makes these goals far more concrete. Remember: As we think, so shall we be. Goal-setting is simply the act of making choices, deciding what we want in our lives and the best way to go about getting it. When our goals are backed by our purpose, we will find a way to accomplish them.

What I like most about goal-setting is that it clarifies for me what I want and don't want. Decision-making becomes easier. When others want me to do something or give them something, if what they want doesn't fit with my goals, it's just so clear that the answer should be no.

Our self-esteem increases as we achieve our goals. We like and respect ourselves more and more, so our attitudes improve and we become more confident people.

Success mapping

Cut out words and pictures of all the things you want to be, to do, and to have; paste them on a big piece of construction paper; and tack it on the wall where you can see it every day. I call this a Success Map. Let it remind you every day of what you're working towards.

Every year for the past 11 years, my business partner, Fiona Carmichael, and I have spent New Year's Eve planning our goals for the coming year. Then we cut out appropriate pictures and paste them on our Success Map. Most years, all the things we have put on our Success Map have come into being by the end of June. We are almost always ahead of our yearly schedule.

One year, I knew I wanted to visit another foreign country, but I couldn't decide which one. Then I saw a beautiful picture of Cairo, the pyramids, and the Sphinx in a travel magazine. I cut it out and pasted it on the month of May on my Success Map. In April, we received a call asking if we would consider going to Egypt in May to conduct a training program. Of course, the answer was yes. And we went first class!

Acting "as if"

When I was a child, my mom would tell me that if I was afraid, I was to act "as if" I were brave. When I lacked confidence, I was to act "as if" I had all the confidence in the world. "Act 'as if' you are the person you want to become," she assured me, "and one day you will discover that 'you are.'"

She was right!

Journaling

Because it takes at least 21 days to change a habit, it is important to document the date when you decide to make a change and why it is that you want to make it. Write in your journal each day, noting what you did that day to effect a desired change, what difficulties you encountered, and what you could do to overcome them. Most importantly, be sure to include your successes.

Gold stars

When I was a kid, my dad was a salesman. Back then, there was no such thing as a daily planner. Dad used a spiral notebook to record his appointments and notes about his customers—what they talked about, what they bought, and when he should call on them again. One day he dropped the notebook on the floor, and I noticed it had gold stars on many of the pages. I remember thinking at the time that for a grown man, putting gold stars in a notebook was a very peculiar thing to do.

When I asked him about it, he smiled and said, "Precious one (he always called me that), sometimes there is too much month left and not enough money. So when I've paid all the bills and provided the best I can for your mother and all of you, I sometimes hear a little voice inside of me that says 'I want something too.' So I've made it a practice of rewarding myself on a daily basis. Doesn't cost much and those gold stars help me to focus on what's going right in my life. Most of all, when I have a bad day, I just flip through my book and I see all those gold stars and think, 'Not every day is so bad. Most days are pretty good.'"

So, for everything that goes right in my day, I put a gold star in my daily planner. For things that turn out exceptionally well, I paste in a whole bunch of gold stars. It keeps me focused on what I did that day and what went right rather than what went wrong. I can flip through my book, watch those stars go zipping by, and instantly remind myself of all the things I am doing right. You'll want to stick some in your journal as well.

Send out the ship

During my childhood, I often heard people dream about what they were going to do when their ship comes in. In other words, what they would do when they got the finances or the wherewithall to do what they really wanted. Overhearing one such comment, my Aunt Meadie asked, "How can they expect their ship to come in when they never sent it out in the first place?"

Wow! If we want to get something out of life, we have to send out the ship: We have to take some kind of positive action to achieve what we want. Success does not come to those who just sit and wait for that proverbial ship. And it certainly does not come to those who sit around being negative and complaining.

Compliment others

Make it a habit to say or do things every single day that will make another person feel better. When you walk past someone, smile and pay them a compliment; make a telephone call to say hello to an elderly person or a friend you haven't spoken to in a while; send a card or an e-mail to someone just to let them know you are thinking of them. It's always the right time to do a kind act.

A trick I use to actually *do* this each day was given me by Fiona Carmichael. She calls it the Five Penny Technique: Put five pennies in your right pocket every morning. Each time you compliment someone (and it has to be an honest compliment), move one penny to your left pocket. Make a commitment not to go home until all five pennies are in your left pocket. It isn't as easy as it sounds. Some nights I've had to stop at the grocery *and* the pharmacy to compliment the clerks just so I could finally go home!

Be kind to yourself

Take the time to discover what you love—what makes your heart sing—then do it on a regular basis. It certainly doesn't have to be profound or complicated: Sit under a tree; lie in the grass and watch the clouds; walk on the beach; go to the library; go to a spa; get a massage; spend time with your family; spend time alone.

Very often we are much nicer to other people than we are to ourselves. The Bible exhorts us to "love thy neighbor as thyself." It does *not* say "*instead of* thyself." You would never say to your best friend, "You're so stupid. You're so dumb. You could have. You should have." Yet how many times have you said exactly those things to yourself?

Stop it. You are never again to follow the words *I am* with a negative word or thought. If you hear yourself doing it, say, "Stop. That's not right." Then say, "I am..." and attach some positive words to it.

Be thankful for your gifts

Every night, when you lay your head on your pillow, say thank you for at least two things in your life for which you are grateful.

On those sometimes difficult nights—when you are laying there thinking about all the things you didn't get done, you still need to do, you could have said, you shouldn't have said, you don't have, and wish you were—concentrate on just two people, traits, or things that happened for which you are grateful. Think about what you *do* have instead of what you don't. Focus on what you *are* instead of what you aren't. As Rev. Robert Schuller tells us, "Obstacles are seldom the same size tomorrow as they are today. Today's responsibilities are tomorrow's possibilities."

I am hoping that you, like Themba, find some meaning in my words and my life lessons. I hope you are able to apply them and find a richer, more purposeful, more joyful life through your choice of a more positive attitude.

I pray you will turn your obstacles into stepping stones and your setbacks into opportunities for growth. I wish you much happiness!

Judi Moreo is an entrepreneur, author, and speaker. Her expertise is in demand by associations, organizations, and corporations worldwide. She has presented programs in 26 countries on four continents. Judi informs, challenges, motivates, and entertains. Most of all, her participants leave with practical, results-oriented techniques to improve both their professional and personal lives.

Prior to becoming a full-time professional speaker, Judi Moreo built a virtual empire from a $2,000 investment, which led the Las Vegas Chamber of Commerce to honor her as Woman of Achievement—Entrepreneur. In 1992, Judi became a Senior Executive in one of South Africa's most prestigious corporations, assisting corporate leaders with the management of change, conflict, and cultural diversity during the abolition of apartheid.

In 1994, she cofounded Turning Point International, a training and development corporation headquartered in Las Vegas, Nevada. She is the coauthor of *Conquer the Brain Drain: 52 Creative Ways to Pump Up Productivity* and *Ignite the Spark: 52 Creative Ways to Boost Productivity*. You can reach Judi at (702) 896-2228. Her Website is *www.turningpointintl.com*

Sharon Spano

COLLECT THE DIAMONDS OF YOUR LIFE

P icture yourself on a serene stretch of beach—feet securely planted, cool white sand fine as baby powder nestled between your toes. Imagine the ocean stretching to the horizon, flat as a glass tabletop, so very much like life—smooth, perfect, nary a ripple. As you lift your right hand to block the sun and look out over the ocean, you note the sparkling reflection. Ah, diamonds, thousands of them, floating on the surface. All you need to do, it seems, is wade out and scoop them up into the palm of your hand.

I can almost hear you grumbling right onto the page: *My life certainly isn't that easy! Sorry, Sharon, you obviously don't have a clue about the pressures I'm under or the stress I feel. You must be talking about someone else's life! And another thing—diamonds don't float. They sink, as any small stone would, directly to the bottom of that ocean. That glimmer is only a reflection on the water, an illusion.*

Your ocean probably isn't so smooth and perfect. Maybe it's more like the battered coast during hurricane season. There you stand, once again, same toes wiggling in that white sand. You're enjoying the moment, your day, your life, when out of nowhere, a storm intervenes. The ocean that only moments before was a serene point of calm in your life now threatens with black horrific waters, waves so high, you dare not venture out. And the diamonds; what of the diamonds? Why, they have all disappeared, just as you'd supposed.

I want you to consider something for just a moment—the diamonds are so obviously an illusion; what if the *storm* is the gift? What if you could learn to accept *every* storm in your life as an invaluable opportunity? Maybe it's only when we confront the storms of our lives that we are forced to take the time to discover what's really important. Are we perhaps missing those dazzling moments of opportunity in our lives simply because we're too busy admiring and reacting to illusions?

I can promise you this: If you stop fighting the harsh reality of your stormy, day-to-day struggle, well, you just might discover that sparkling gem after all—that one diamond, in all its perfection, intended just for you.

You Can Survive the Storms

Did you notice that no matter what's happening on the surface of those waters, no matter how torrential the rains, or the size of the waves, the bottom of the ocean remains relatively calm and stable? That's where we need to be as individuals, stable and constant enough within our own lives—at the very core of who we are—to survive whatever storms life has in store for us.

How do we do that? How do we survive, yet alone thrive, during the day-to-day struggles we all must face?

Simply stated, we must commit to a plan of action that allows us to balance mind, body, and spirit. For purposes of this chapter, I'd like to focus on Mind Balance, the process through which we can develop more awareness of our own thoughts, moment by moment. Doing so will naturally allow us to become more present in the moment, more creative, and more responsive—rather than reactive—to life's challenges.

Like most of you, I've survived a few major storms. Allow me to share a few of the diamonds I've picked up along the way.

Rise Above the Moment

Mind Balance requires "thought presence" in the moment. Whenever I'm engaged in a conversation, situation, or event, I've conditioned my mind to consciously rise above that moment. When I do so, it's as if I'm the director of a movie peering through a camera lens. I am completely detached from whatever is going on. I can hear my own voice directing thought and behavior, carefully instructing me. In Eckhart Tolle's best-selling *The Power of Now*, this process of "mind watching" is extolled as a way to enlightened consciousness.

Most of the time, we are so completely paralyzed by the many thoughts that bombard our minds—and the fact that we define ourselves by them—it is difficult to separate ourselves from them. By practicing "mind awareness," we can learn to reach higher levels of Mind Balance.

There's no trick to this process. Start by paying attention to what goes on in your head. How do you *think* about the moments and events in your life? Just notice your thoughts, like an objective movie director, free of judgment. What thoughts do you have when you're engaged in stressful situations? When your mother-in-law unexpectedly shows up at the front door? When you have a flat tire? When your boss is demanding you do 72 things at once?

Watch for Dark Clouds

Once you become practiced at "mind watching," you can then begin to make different choices about what thoughts to engage in. Yes, you can choose your thoughts.

Let's exercise the mind for a moment with a little game. Close your eyes for a second and try to capture a thought—any thought—before it disappears. Don't get discouraged if you don't manage to do it right away. Most of our thoughts tend to whiz through our minds at supersonic speed! Take a deep breath and try to hold onto one thought for just a moment. Got it? Okay, now imagine that thought encased in a fluffy white cloud. Hold onto it a little longer. Now, let the cloud go. Watch it float away, just like a cloud moving across the sky on a windy day. Then, *poof!*, it's gone. Now, choose another thought, and place it in another white cloud. Then, again, let it go.

This practice is a double-edged sword, teaching you how to let your thoughts go *and* how to *choose* which ones you will keep around. Unfortunately, when we're out of balance in our lives, we tend to grab onto negative thoughts. You know them—they're the ones encased in those black clouds. We let them in, then hold onto them so tightly that they define the way we think. They define our entire attitude. The next thing you know, your mind is repeating the negativity over and over again: *I'll never have a decent relationship in my life. I'll never get that promotion. I don't deserve to be treated better.*

If you think any thought long enough, it starts to become truth—at least in your own mind—and you start to take action based on the perceived reality of that thought. That action then determines an outcome that supports the negative thought. Congratulations! You have now succeeded in creating a negative *reality*.

Here's the secret: Practice letting the dark cloud go just the way you did the white cloud. Watch it move on through your mind. Choose a white cloud instead, one that says *I deserve to have a loving relationship in my life. I should get that promotion. I am good enough.*

See how easy it is? Choose your thoughts. Shift your attitude. Change your life.

Expect Changes In the Weather

It is much easier to choose your thoughts if you accept the fact that life is circumstantial—it changes like the weather. Just when you think you've got it all figured out, everything spins in another direction. The easiest way to move with this current of change is simply to accept it as reality. Yes, I know you'd like to think that everything that happens to *you* is really significant, but the truth is that life is nothing more than a series of circumstances. We often find ourselves in situations—storms, if you will—that we have no control over. You've been fired. You've recently lost a loved one, or, God forbid, the high school principal has just phoned to tell you that your son—yes, *your* little darling—has been arrested for selling drugs.

Stuff happens, storms pop up unexpectedly, and though we often don't have a choice about what happens to us, we do have a choice about how we *think* about those circumstances.

Let me share with you a brief story about how I learned this lesson...the very hard way.

"Something is wrong with the baby!"

April 3, 1981. Those six little words rocked my world.

I was 29 years old, married seven years, and we were ready, oh, so ready for this baby. We had waited until the house, the car, and our careers were all in place. Then, without warning, a giant wave knocked us upside down and sideways.

"Something is wrong with the baby!"

A heart condition, they said. We'd like to do some tests. Everything will be fine.

I won't bore you with the gory details of those first few months. We did survive. And the baby—Michael—seemed to have weathered his own first storm.

When Michael was 10 months old, as my husband and I were preparing to move from Los Angeles to Orlando—the moving van was literally in my driveway—the phone rang. It was Dr. Gordon, my son's cardiologist.

"Mrs. Spano, I'm afraid I can't let you take Michael to Florida without further testing," he said. "The results of his last physical have come back. We're dealing with something far more serious than a heart condition."

Dr. Gordon had decided to call in a leading neurologist to perform a muscle biopsy at Children's Hospital and wanted to know if we could be there next Tuesday.

Days later, my husband and I sat in the waiting room, no words between us. The air was tight, the way I imagined a casket might feel. The room was empty except for two small chairs facing a third, and a small box of tissues on a nearby table. This is a room where tears flow, I thought to myself.

Finally, footsteps outside the doorway, and Dr. Gordon entered the room, dark eyes cold with sadness. He evidently told us quite a bit, but I only remember a single sentence: "If you're lucky," he intoned, "Michael may live until the age of 2."

For one moment, I was fully aware of my husband's 180-pound body sitting beside me. Then he seemed to float upward from his seat, like a huge balloon, until, as with the prick of a pin, *whoosh*, he deflated and fell into a puddle of nothingness onto the floor beside me. I was alone in that room, and there was a stranger with sad brown eyes sitting directly across from me, telling me that my 10-month-old baby was going to die.

I quickly realized in that moment that if I was going to have the strength to survive this, if I was going to be what I needed to be for my husband and my son, if I was going to get Michael the services he needed, I was going to have to reinvent myself and how I dealt with my life.

I was going to have to learn new and confusing terminology. I was going to have to learn to be a better communicator—to listen and ask intelligent questions. I was going to have to learn everything I could about medicine and education and therapy and...I was going to have to do anything and everything I could to keep my son alive.

That moment of insanity—that most profound circumstance— began my 22-year journey into the realm of thought and life balance.

I spent the first four years of my son's life thinking about his impending death. Then, on one stormy morning that seemed darker than all the rest, as I stood frozen outside his doorway, hand on the knob, preparing myself, as I did each morning, for the possibility that this might be the day I would find his lifeless body, I made a decision.

What if I thought differently about this most challenging circumstance? What if I decided to focus on the quality of life each day rather than Michael's death? How might that change the things I said and did? How might this single shift in my thinking impact the way I loved and cared for my child?

This shift in thought—in attitude—was the beginning of a completely new way of life. Sometimes, I learned, you have to accept what *is*, before you can do anything about what *isn't*. Before I could engage in positive choice of thought, before I could begin to shift to a mindset of white clouds, I had to accept my life's circumstance. I had to move outside the paralysis of fearful thinking to an understanding that, although I could not "fix" the circumstances of my life, I did have a choice about how I thought about them. If I changed my thinking, I could experience different results.

As I look back over the last 22 years of my son's life, I realize how fortunate I was to have made that choice of acceptance. I said earlier that sometimes the storm is the gift. And, yes, Michael is the most challenging circumstance of my life. He is confined to a wheelchair and requires care 24 hours a day, seven days a week. He has limited use of his hands, poor speech articulation, and limited vision. As you might imagine, we have undergone many storms. But it is precisely those storms that have forced us to a much more powerful level of conscious thought.

In spite of Michael's many physical challenges, he has had a life filled with love, passion, and adventure. He truly is the diamond that keeps me grounded in Mind Balance.

Reprogram Your Computer

Once you've learned to watch your thoughts, accept your circumstances, and engage in choice of thought, how do you sustain Mind Balance?

Remember the old adage: Your thoughts become your words. Your words become your actions. Your actions shape your character. And your character is your destiny.

What this means is that we must not only be aware of our thoughts in order to make better choices about which to "engage," we have to be discerning about what information we let into our minds in the first place. Just like a computer: Garbage in, garbage out. If all I'm putting into my mental computer is negative information, what will come out of the computer when I'm under stress is negative thought, negative talk, and negative action. The result? A life overflowing with negativity.

Avoid the Toxic Media

Much of what we read, see, and hear is intended to sell us something, probably something we neither need nor want. It is often information that is sensationalized, dramatized, and designed to make us fear and worry. If this is what we are putting into our mental computer, that's what will come out when we face one of our storms. We must pay closer attention to what we watch, read, and listen to.

We must decide to eliminate clutter from our minds. Be more discerning about the things we read—choose literature that is wholesome, inspirational, or instructional. Avoid news and movies that are overly dramatic and unnecessarily violent. We don't have to be prudish about such things, but we *can* be more discriminating about what we allow into our computer.

Clearly, it is our responsibility to keep up with current events, but we can choose the highest forms of journalism, the best books and magazines. We can engage in entertaining and informative types of theater. We can choose to enlighten our minds with art and music. We can choose the silence of an afternoon walk on a spring day. We can choose to enjoy a song of peace over the drama of misery.

Avoid Toxic People

Who are toxic people? All of those friends, relatives, and colleagues who want to pull you into the dramatic storms of their lives. They never seem to be enough or *have* enough. They consistently engage in negative action and behavior: the coworker who complains about her raise; the father-in-law who whines through a gourmet meal; the child who is never satisfied. They have chronic backaches, headaches, and are always tired of something. In short, they are people who live out of balance in their lives, and every time you try to move forward, they seem to suck the energy right out of you and pull you back down into the muck.

If you can't physically remove yourself from their all-consuming presence, at least attempt to separate yourself from them mentally and emotionally. This is a topic that we can't possibly discuss in detail in this short chapter, but, at the very least, I am asking you to shift your thinking, to understand that we *cannot* change these people. What we *can* do is develop strategies to insulate ourselves from their negativity. We can learn how to cope with them, doing the best we can to interact or get the job done in spite of who they are—husbands, wives, friends, bosses, kids.

Once we become more balanced in Mind, Body, and Spirit, we may develop more patience with these challenging individuals, but until such time, simply avoid them. As one of my closest friends likes to remind me: If you lie down with dogs, you will inevitably wake up with fleas.

Ride the Perfect Storm

Many of us are too often filled with doubts about our performance and whether we have achieved success, whether we've become "all that we can be." Others unconsciously sabotage our efforts by procrastinating, failing to meet deadlines and objectives, breaking our word. On the other extreme, some of us hold ourselves to impossible standards, overcommit our time, and *still* believe we never do enough. Our fears and doubts keep us from experiencing fulfillment. The result is that we never give ourselves credit for getting through the storm.

Riding the perfect storm means to focus on excellence rather than perfection, to perform to our utmost capability without sabotaging our chances for success or expecting more than is humanly possible. It is accomplishing a task or achieving an objective with the understanding that as long as you do your best with integrity, you have done enough.

I put this diamond in my pocket when my son was 5 years old. Before that time, I was a woman who suffered from perfectionism. Every moment of each day was planned out. I was a slave to my day planner! One friend teased me without mercy because my pantry was color-coded, with cereal boxes in alphabetical order.

Then it happened. I was looking forward to that week between Christmas and New Year's. I was going to get the house back together, catch up on all that reading, start the New Year in perfect order. But Michael had other plans. He suddenly came down with a fever of 104 degrees. Without warning, we found ourselves in the hospital for the entire week. Suddenly none of those things on my schedule mattered. The only thing that mattered was getting Michael well and home again.

Worry about things that *really* matter. When you're in the middle of the perfect storm and the ship seems likes it's going down, don't worry about mopping the deck. Michael taught me that there is no such thing as perfectionism. If I have limited time, limited resources, and limited energy, I do my very best in the now and move on.

Seek Out a Safe Port

Last but not least, we must make time to move beyond thought to a "quiet mind." A quiet mind has the potential to rekindle spirit and to nurture the body in ways that unravel stress. Unfortunately, too many of us tend to have minds cluttered with noise. We are addicted to thinking, our minds overflowing with the busy traffic of noisy "to-dos" and "have-tos." The harder we try to quiet our minds, the more thoughts seem to rush in.

In the early years of my son's illness, I learned that I had a "busy" mind, endlessly filled with worry. This is not a condition that occurs overnight. For me, it had developed from years of sprinting through life—from work to home and back again, two hectic environments of deadlines, details, and dilemmas. I used to proudly state that our calendar was "booked" four months in advance, each weekend overflowing with activity, never a moment to rest. It wasn't too long after Michael's birth before I realized that I did not have the clarity of thought to make solid decisions. The worry was so intense, I had trouble sleeping and often found myself thinking long into the early morning hours, leaving me exhausted as the new day began.

For me, the way to a quiet mind was to engage in a disciplined practice of prayer and meditation. I literally had to train my mind to shut off. I began a specific practice of meditation—20 minutes, twice daily. What I discovered astonished me. Not only did my mind begin to slow down, but my creativity began to heighten. I moved through day-to-day interactions with less anxiety. The many stressful situations in my life just didn't seem to be as stressful. My thoughts calmed down, no longer rushing in one after another in a traffic jam of activity. Rather, each thought was more like a single car on a leisurely afternoon drive up the avenue. I became more focused and tolerant of the annoying aspects of my day. I began to make better choices.

Because I believe meditation is a very personal thing and that each person must discover what is right for her, I won't be so presumptuous as to tell you "how" to meditate. I would, however, like to offer a few supporting thoughts as to "why."

For many years, meditation has been researched and supported by the National Institutes of Health as an alternative approach to wellness. The first book I ever read on meditation was *The Relaxation Response* by Dr. Herbert Benson. Because of his early work and the ongoing research of NIH, we now know that meditation can reduce stress in the body, lower risk for heart disease and specific cancers, and be instrumental in reducing or even eliminating chronic pain. I believe it is one of the most important things a woman can do for herself. It's free, requires very little time, can be done anywhere...and the benefits are endless.

Enjoy the Journey

Finally, the most important thing to remember in trying to achieve Mind Balance is that *it's a process*. Small incremental changes over time can create extraordinary results. Don't try to implement every idea at once. Begin to take note of your own thoughts, and be kind to yourself when you notice that you're thinking or reacting in negative ways. With that first moment of awareness comes opportunity for change.

Imagine yourself once again at the bottom of that ocean, the storm above you rising, and in the midst of it, you discover the greatest diamond of all: Where you are is exactly where you're supposed to be. Even in the midst of those murky waters, there exist diamonds of opportunity. Every life circumstance, every challenge and storm, has its purpose. We need only embrace the option to discover and learn. We need only choose to see that each storm is an opportunity to move to higher levels of consciousness and Mind Balance.

With each diamond of discovery comes the promise of passion, greater clarity of thought, and a life that sparkles with joy.

I wish you all of that and more!

Sharon Spano is president of Spano & Company, Inc., a professional development company based in Orlando, Florida. As an experienced consultant specializing in training and development, she has empowered corporate leaders across North America to increase employee potential, maximize performance, and improve bottom-line results.

Sharon's clients include Johns Hopkins University, MIT, Bell South, Sara Lee Branded Apparel, and the United States Navy. Her unique approach to leadership development—with emphasis on integrity in the workplace—has successfully helped such companies reestablish a corporate culture where continuous improvement, higher levels of achievement, standards of excellence, and increased customer satisfaction are the norm rather than the exception.

As a professional speaker committed to excellence, Sharon's seminars and keynote addresses have inspired audiences from all walks of life. Her primary focus is getting people to do more (improve productivity) as they simultaneously develop an insatiable desire for life balance and continued growth and development.

She is the author of the internationally distributed CD series How to Handle Conflict and Confrontation. Her most recent publication, *Magnetic Leadership*, emphasizes how to get results in corporate America.

She may be contacted at Spano & Company, Inc., 649 Stonefield Loop, Heathrow, Florida 32746. Phone: (407) 333.0224; Fax: (407) 444.3840; or on the Web at *www.sharonspano.com*.

Success
of the
Soul

Leanne Mackenzie

YOU'VE JUST GOTTA LAUGH

As I begin this chapter about humor and stress, I realize that my recent travel experience might just be the perfect example of what humor is all about for today's working woman.

Allow me to explain. Last night, I returned home from a business trip. The plane was delayed two hours because of weather. The delay caused me to miss a family birthday party that I had been really looking forward to because I was finally going to have a couple of hours of interaction with people I know and like.

Through the plane ride home, my feet started to swell, as they seem prone to doing ever since I reached age 40. The book I was reading, although humorous, seemed a little too close to reality for me. The flight attendant was a kindred spirit and could sense that I was a road warrior at the end of the battle. This earned me four packages of pretzels.

When I finally arrived at the airport, my husband was waiting for me at the baggage claim, not looking terribly happy. The airline had not given him the correct information on my arrival time. We both needed dinner but neither of us had the energy to bother making anything. Before heading to bed, I had a stale roll and a glass of milk—a far cry from the lamb I had two nights earlier at the Swissotel in Boston.

The next day, Saturday, started with a lonesome golden retriever butting her head into my hand at 5 a.m. I tried to ignore her, but having been gone for five days necessitated that I give her some attention. I went downstairs and discovered a house that had been neglected—newspapers not out of their plastic wraps, mail unopened, cans and unwashed glasses on the counter.

I decided to turn my attention to catching up on my e-mails and headed to my home office. When I found that, once again, my son or daughter (each blames the other) had tampered with the computer, causing all e-mail access to be unavailable, I began to cry.

I had promised a client in Boston that I would have a proposal to her on Monday. All of our correspondence had been via e-mail, so I didn't even have a phone number or address available that was not locked up inside my computer. My husband finished retrieving at least the current e-mails just in time for me to go pick up my daughter Emily from her sleepover. How can we see this as anything *but* humorous?

The ironic part of all of this is that this kind of situation is becoming routine.

The juggling act that professional women perform every single day is a true work of art. So how do we keep our sanity under control and our sense of humor intact? By following the seven principles listed here:

I. Flexibility

Here's my theory on flexibility: You must be more organized at home and less organized at work. Why? Because we need to be flexible in today's workplace, which allows us to be team players, something that is so coveted today. Quite often, extreme organization makes us appear inflexible. It can also lead us to believe that there is only one right answer, one correct way of doing things. This way of thinking is not highly valued in today's workplace.

Part of the reason that we want things done "our way" is because we are under a tremendous amount of pressure to accomplish tasks in both our professional and personal lives. We need to make sure that our personal lives are organized so that we can leave them behind both mentally and physically when we walk out the door to work. Being able to compartmentalize our lives allows us to focus on the professional when we are at work, and the personal when we're home, enabling us to accomplish so much more without being overwhelmed by the stress of handling both worlds at once.

2. Give Up Control

Giving up control is perhaps the best thing we can do to reduce the most stress. It is also the hardest of the seven tips to accomplish.

The truth is, we like completion. We like to stroke things off our to-do list, sometimes *so* much that we add items to that list just for the sake of completing more tasks.

Instead, what we need to do is to change our perception of tasks and our need to complete more. We should tackle the big things first, not (as most of us do) the little ones. When we arrive at the office in the morning, our first inclination—after taking off our coats and getting our coffee—is to pick up our voice mail and e-mail messages. Already, the whole day's organization is lost because we are now off and running to complete the little things.

What we need to do—even if only for 10 minutes—is to start on those big projects. As we age, many of us become morning people— we do our best work first thing in the morning. But we are wasting our best energy on little tasks, which only makes those big projects more stress-filled when we finally get to them at the end of the day. They have been sitting on the desk all day stressing us out. Therefore, if we work on the big projects for even 10 minutes, we will have the motivation needed to continue. And because most of us are "completionists," we will finish them.

3. Be Open to Change

The word *change* used to inspire excitement of the unknown: Something different was about to happen, something that was going to make life more exciting. In the past few years, this word has taken on a different connotation. Many organizations announced layoffs, telling the remaining staff they'd have to do the work of their former coworkers—without pay raises—a situation they should look upon as an "opportunity for growth." Daring to dissent from this corporate mentality meant that you were inflexible, not open to change, and ultimately, not a team player.

I believe one of the reasons change seems to be so debilitating is that it strips us of the control over our own lives. In the workplace, we have a certain amount of control. We must be able to set limits and have them respected. There is only so much work that we are physically capable of, and we must communicate these limits to those whose expectations are sometimes unrealistic. In our personal lives, though, we often set our own unreasonable expectations. To enjoy change, we must realize that we are not capable of changing all aspects of our lives at once, but instead approach change in stages, so we avoid causing ourselves major stress.

4. Maintain a Stress Balance

Maintaining a stress balance works as a seesaw does: We must be creative about reducing our stress, and we must reduce stress to remain creative.

No matter how many self-help books you read, the reality of stress reduction comes down to finding very personal ways of dealing with it, ways that are unique to your problems. You cannot use someone else's solutions. You may adapt ideas, but ultimately, you have to come up with your own plan of action.

Let's take a look at some of the major causes of stress. That's where we'll find solutions that, for most of us, may include conflict resolution, life planning, problem solving, and self-nourishment.

◆ **Conflict Resolution.** In *The Seven Habits of Highly Effective People*, author Stephen Covey says that insanity is doing the same thing over and over again and expecting different results. And yet every day, we walk into the office and try to deal with people in the same ineffective manner that failed yesterday. There are three ways to deal with conflict:

1. You can meet it head-on, which is what most resolvable conflict needs. Many of us are uncomfortable dealing with people in this way. However, without discussing the problem and ways to solve it, it will simply remain. By meeting it head-on, we also don't allow the emotion to build up. No conflict is solvable when one or both parties are emotional.

2. We can let it go. This is a remarkably difficult solution for a great many women who feel that it is *their* responsibility to carry the burden of a difficult person or relationship. I want you to ask yourself: *What is in this relationship for me?* If you honestly answer *nothing,* perhaps it is time to let the relationship or conflict go.

3. The third way to resolve conflict is to get out of the situation. Many people stay in situations of unsolvable conflict for too long. The only person's behavior we can change is our own. If the situation is not solvable, perhaps a change in yourself is in order.

◆ **Life planning**, or more specifically the lack of life planning, is also a huge stressor. Every day, I meet women who have let a bad day completely derail their lives. Women with a life plan consider a bad day just a bump in the road, because they know where they are going. It is those who have fallen into a career and are not looking forward to what they would like to do next who are lost. Examine *your* situation. Do you know where you're going? What do you need to do to get there? Are you improving yourself and your skills? Every person in the workplace should be updating his or her resume every six months. If you haven't done something new to add to your resume in the last six months, you are becoming stale. Build your life plan, then put it into action.

◆ **Problem solving** is the biggest stress reducer of all. Every day that I am out speaking to people, I meet women who want to share their problems...but don't want to listen to suggestions on improving their situations. To be able to look at a problem and see potential solutions gives our lives an outward focus. Once we act on our potential solutions, we confirm that we really do have control over our personal happiness.

◆ **Self-nourishment.** If we really want to reduce our stress, we must find the things that will help us. This is different for every person. Perhaps you'd like to go back to school, work out, relax in a bathtub, sip a glass of wine, chat quietly with your best friend, read the paper with a good cup of coffee, go whitewater rafting, or just read a good book. Stress is personal and so are the solutions to it. Each person must be responsible for her own self-nourishment plan.

5. Be a Creative Problem-solver

Working women are experts on creative solutions. We are capable of organizing, minimizing, and optimizing just about every situation we encounter—that is, until we are stressed. Stress is the biggest creativity block that we encounter. As working women, we must keep up our creative solutions to life's problems. In this time of unemployment and layoffs, we must keep looking for extraordinary solutions. No one is about to give us more money to do our jobs, nor are our bosses going to come to us and reduce our ever-increasing workloads. We are responsible for solving these problems. It is up to us to come up with the creative solutions they demand.

Fortunately, women are well equipped to handle this task. The key is to become comfortable sharing our creative solutions. Problem-solving is one of the key ways that management today measures performance. We need to get the ideas out there.

6. Network for Support

Networking is a vital weapon in the working woman's arsenal. We need to know that other women have the same dilemmas we do. Who do you talk to regarding issues at work? Do you have someone with whom you can talk and who understands your specific problems? Someone who can guide you along the right path? We each need someone who can provide us with encouragement and guidance. This person needs to have an awareness of our situation and insight into potential creative solutions.

7. Seek Out the Humor

No matter how you go about it, I strongly advise that you find a way to reduce your stress and to have a good laugh. Humorous situations don't tend to happen while you are relaxing in a lounge chair on a cruise ship; they usually happen during our everyday encounters with others. You are responsible for your own actions, and actions are necessary for humor and for stress reduction. Humor and stress will always be with us, but if you can combine the two, you will find that the working woman's life is truly an interesting and fulfilling one.

Leanne Mackenzie has been making people laugh in her vocation as a motivational speaker since 1999. Often compared to a young version of Erma Bombeck, Leanne's humor revolves around the common, everyday things that all of us experience. Men and women alike enjoy her unique style of training and motivation.

Leanne believes that humor and creativity go hand in hand. In the last year, she has spent a great deal of time overseeing creativity training for aging Baby Boomers who are struggling with careers that require too much effort and deliver too little fun.

She owns her own training and consulting company, MACS (Mackenzie's Academic Consulting Service). She holds a BAA from Ryerson University in Toronto, a B.Ed. from the University of Toronto, and a Masters in Education from Brock University.

Originally from Canada, Leanne now resides in Chicago with Andy, her husband of 18 years, and Drew and Emily, her two children. You can learn more about Leanne and MACS at her Website, *www.leannemackenzie.com.*

Jan Elliott

HELPING OUR DAUGHTERS TO GROW

Daughters are precious gifts from God. When I was given my baby girl, I gave her the name Allison. Her middle name was Louise, the same as mine, her grandmother's, and her great-grandmother's. She had big green eyes, and her hair looked like it would become a dark strawberry blonde. She favored her father in looks more than her mother.

But she was clearly *my* little angel. What a beautiful thing to have a daughter who loved to be with her mother! She became my constant shadow, my little friend. She loved clothes, dressing up, makeup, shopping, dolls, tea parties—many of the same things I loved. She began helping me in the kitchen, later baking cookies and making simple treats for the family. She seemed to really enjoy all the same things I enjoyed.

How could she not be just like me?

Then she began elementary school, and things began to change. Her teachers said she seemed shy and didn't make friends easily. Sometimes, they said, it was hard for her to join a larger group. She also rarely raised her hand in class or contributed any information, ideas, or suggestions.

I found that very hard to believe! After all, she was MY daughter. I was confident, self-assured, and felt that if I put my mind to it, I could do anything. I joined in, took the lead, had ideas, suggestions. I was never afraid to speak up. Perhaps she just needed encouragement, someone to push her—to help her realize she *did* have good ideas and *could* be a leader. But whenever I would try to encourage her, she would just say, "I don't want to, Mommy. I don't want to raise my hand or be first in line."

I would say, "Of course you do, you are my daughter!" And then she would cry. Now, that certainly was no reason to cry. You should save those tears for the big stuff, I thought.

When she was 9 years old, our family moved to Washington State. I loved moving! To me, it meant new adventures, new friends, a new career. We moved into a new neighborhood only to discover that the family next door had a daughter named Allison, too, a little girl the same age as our Allison. Perfect, I thought, a new friend right next door! Her mother and I became friends; the dads even played golf together.

The Effect We Have on Our Daughters

Around us, the "new" Allison (Allison M.) was great, and she and our Allison seemed to get along. But at school, it was a different story. Allison M. and her friends had been together since kindergarten, and our Allison was excluded from their clique. Allison M. often said nasty, cruel things, and accused our Allison of being a liar and a "copycat."

And guess what? Whenever my Allison would tell me about something hateful and cruel that Allison M. had done, I never believed her. Instead, I would accuse her! "It must be your fault," I would say. "What are you doing to cause the other girls to dislike you? How can you not want to play with that sweet girl from right next door?"

Our Allison began to be very mean and verbally abusive to her younger brother, Josh. She'd often take out her frustrations by hitting and slapping him. We would punish her and send her to her room, but nothing seemed to help. What I didn't know was that she would beat him more when we were not home. He never told us about this; he was afraid she would beat him even more. I wonder where her frustration came from?

After three long years, our family moved again, this time to central Illinois. Allison would now attend a smaller school, which I thought would be to her advantage. She quickly made friends with Amy and Mandy, two girls from her new neighborhood. The three girls bonded instantly. I believed things were changing for the better. The girls tried out for Flag Corps, and all three made the team. Already it seemed like a much better year!

Then, in their freshmen year of high school, the girls decided to try out for cheerleading—and I'll bet you can guess what happened next. Amy and Mandy made the squad. Allison did not. She was very good at the tryouts, but forgot to smile—that really big smile that the judges look for. That was another let-down, and another let-down was not what she needed for her self-esteem and self-confidence.

The year progressed and we were relocated again, this time to Pittsburgh, Penn. Allison was enrolled in a very large school. There would be 1,200 students in just her 9th and 10th grade building, another 1,200 students in the 11th and 12th grades. It was very difficult for her to make friends and get involved in school activities. At one parent-teacher conference in the 10th grade, her teacher mentioned to me what a lovely, beautiful girl Allison was. It was hard to believe, she added, that she had such low self-esteem.

Low self-esteem? *Low self-esteem?* My daughter? I hardly knew what the term meant! Here I thought she was just shy and didn't push herself—so unlike her mother.

Allison became friends with a girl who was her age, but acted years older. I think Allison was attracted to her because this girl "knew no boundaries." She encouraged Allison to try many new things—most of them bad—and even persuaded her to skip school. (I only found out about this when the school had an evening open house and several of the teachers commented on her absence, an absence that was news to me.) There were several more such incidents, and finally we told her she could not be friends with that girl anymore.

As she began to mature and to become more beautiful inside and out, it seemed harder and harder for her to make friends with the opposite sex. She was very shy and bashful if a boy so much as spoke to her. At the same time, her own dad seemed to pull away. His little daughter had become a beautiful young woman, and he didn't quite know how to handle that. This only made it more difficult for her to figure out how to interact with young men. She didn't even receive an invitation to her own junior prom, and spent the evening working at her part-time job at Baskin–Robbins.

The Importance of Self-esteem

Well, we made it through those high school years. Allison's mother—yes, that would be me—just didn't understand how important it was in life to have the self-confidence and self-esteem she pretty much took for granted. And how hard it is for someone who doesn't.

Nathaniel Branden writes in his book, *The Psychology of Self-Esteem*, "There is no value judgment more important to man—no factor more decisive in his psychological development and motivation—than the estimate he places on himself."

What causes low self-esteem? Perhaps it is a lack of meaning or purpose; not having faith in yourself; or feeling dependent on others, especially your mother, for approval or recognition. Does it ever come naturally? I don't believe so—you are not born with negative or positive self-esteem. You learn it along the way. Low self-esteem is a direct result of the way the significant adults in your life treat you, especially during your formative years.

Dr. Robert Schuller has his own thoughts on where such a poor self-image originates: "You are not what *you* think you are, you are not what *I* think you are, you are what you think I think you are." Our Allison spent those tough years in the 4th, 5th, and 6th grades thinking she was who Allison M. thought she was.

Glenn Van Ekeren applies Dr. Schuller's observation to the story of Cinderella, who was trapped in a lifestyle that her mean ol' step-sisters *told* her she was in. They laughed at the thought of Cinderella going to the ball, so eventually even Cinderella considered it a ludicrous dream. Like Cinderella, we often receive our self-image from those around us. It is not necessarily what they think of us, but what *we think they think* of us that influences our own self-image.

It is not just us parents who are to blame.

Don't you wish more teachers had higher self-esteem and knew how to pass it on to our children in the classroom? After all, they are the second most important influence on our children's lives.

Wouldn't it be great if our kids' coaches knew how to really build self-esteem? Shouldn't our kids learn how to affirm themselves in the face of degrading, hurtful remarks? How beneficial would that be to our children? To our daughters? I heard a story about a football coach, frustrated during a practice, who screamed out: "All of you dumbbells go take a shower!" All but one player ran quickly into the locker room. Angered by what he thought was an act of insubordination, the coach charged up to the player and growled, "Well?" But the young man just stood there and chuckled as he replied, "There certainly were a lot of them, weren't there, Coach?"

So How Do We Develop Our Own Self-esteem?

In addition to what everybody else has to say to us and about us, what we say to ourselves significantly impacts how we see ourselves. We have more than 50,000 conversations with ourselves every day. Are they positive conversations? Are they building up our own self-images or tearing them to bits? How you deal with that little voice whispering inside your head has a great deal to do with your own self-esteem. The battlefield is really in your mind.

So we all have to learn how to replace negative messages with positive ones. All positive self-talk messages begin with the word "I." They are all in the present tense. And they are all positive! Write a series of simple statements, such as *I am worthy, I am powerful, I am good at what I do.* Or, as suggested in *The Psychology of Achievement* by Brain Tracy: *I like me. I like me. I like me.* Place these little statements everywhere—the bathroom mirror, the dashboard of your car, inside closets. They need to be read every day—many, many *times* every day. Otherwise, as motivational speaker Gail Cohen says, "The reason most people don't accomplish their goals or change their way of thinking is because they live on an island. It's called Someday I'll..."

Seek out relationships with people who are interested in helping you bring out the best in yourself. And be the kind of mother who gives her daughter the positive messages she so desperately needs. As motivational speaker Les Brown puts it: "It's not what you give your children that matters, it's what you leave in them that counts." The power of self-esteem is one of the greatest gifts you can give your children.

If Only I Had Known

These are the things I would have taught my daughter, had I understood better all those years. I would have:

- offered more words of encouragement.
- sought more ways to help her believe in herself.
- helped her to become more assertive.
- let her speak up more, let her tell others what she wanted, even just let her order in a restaurant. I always felt I had to do it for her, giving her the impression (I see now) that she was not able or capable. There were so many opportunities to let her speak for and stand up for herself, opportunities I never gave her.
- been more accepting.
- shown her God's unconditional love for her.
- realized that although she was my daughter, she was not like me. And I would have been okay with that.

I am happy to say that as I finally began to learn these things, Allison was about to graduate from college. I have now been able to pass these and many other insights on to her. Her father also began to mentor and guide her through her college years, building a relationship that has helped her handle her relationships with young men. As Maya Angelou once said: "You did what you knew. And then when you knew better, you did better."

Because of the mentoring and guidance she has received from her family, new business acquaintances, and new friends, Alison has matured into a beautiful, self-assured young women.

Here's the process I would have followed had I known then what I know now. If you follow these steps, I know you will have success instilling self-esteem in your daughter:

- *Hold your tongue.* You do not have to comment on every decision she makes.
- *Be accepting of her appearance.* Don't try to make her into something she is not. You do not have to have—or voice—an opinion on how she should wear her hair or the clothes she chooses. Let her develop her own style.
- *Praise her more.* Tell her you are proud of her at least once a day.
- *Find something she is good at* and encourage her to do it more.
- *Teach her to pray.* God hears all prayers and will answer.
- *Encourage a strong, healthy relationship* with her father and/ or grandfather.
- *Teach her positive self-talk,* such as, "I like me. I accept myself unconditionally."
- *Help to reprogram her mind* by concentrating on positive thoughts the first and last moment of each day. These are powerful golden moments.
- *Listen to what is being said and meant.* Women have an innate ability to read between the lines. Make sure you take time to listen—it's the most important way to build a lasting relationship.

It's never too late or too early to start. And it is the greatest gift you will ever give your daughter.

Allison recently said to me, "Mother, I just wanted you to be proud of me." I was *always* proud of her. She just never knew it, because I did not say it enough or show it enough. Self-esteem is a powerful thing. You can't give it to your daughters if you don't have it yourself. In my case, I had it to give; I just didn't know how. And now that I do...I do.

Jan may be reached through her Website, *www.janspeaks.com.*

JoAnn Corley

SAFE PLACE, SACRED SPACE

It was a late Saturday evening in June, 2000, as I laid my head onto the pillow in the bedroom adjacent to my mother's. I was hoping she would have a restful night after another day of wrestling with the reality that she was in the final stage of breast cancer, with no treatments left to try. During this period, I would come over during part of the week and on weekends to care for her, as did my dad and older brother, and would sleep in my old bedroom next to hers.

This day was particularly difficult as we worked through my first time caring for her in intimate ways that challenged her sense of privacy and dignity. She was embarrassed as I offered to clean an "accident," and we talked through how I felt about being able to help, how much it meant to me, and how appropriate my helping in this way was.

After she let me help, she lay back down, clean and at peace. I excused myself, made my way to the bathroom, and buried my head in a bunch of towels and sobbed. Having a strong, independent, outspoken mother reduced to wearing diapers was more than I could bear.

As I lay in bed that night, my heart was filled with so much pain, I thought it was going to burst. Where would I find the strength to make it though this? To be there for her in the ways that she needed? Where could I find the capabilities to make each of her dying days meaningful and memorable, and filled with joy, laughter, and peace for both her and my dad?

My life was all over the place at this point. I was commuting back and forth between my parents' house and mine, while trying to continue my own life, connect with my husband and friends, run my consulting business, and go to church when I could.

What would keep me sane and refreshed during this most difficult, stressful time?

One thing was for sure: prayer. It had to be! Now, I know this word scares some people. Sometimes our preconceived notions can even prevent us from embracing new experiences. But there are many meanings and experiences associated with the word. I think this time with my mother forced me out of my own previously held notions about prayer.

As my head sunk into the pillows that night, I began to move into that quiet mode. Usually, when it comes time for me to pray, I have plenty to say. That night, nothing. Everything had already spilled out through my tears onto the bathroom towels earlier in the day. I was feeling such a deep sense of losing the mom I knew, my heart was breaking—I was speechless.

That night I learned that even if you have no words to say, you can still pray—prayer can be silence.

As the role of caregiver began to take its toll, I barely had enough energy to get out of my clothes at the end of the day. I would fall into bed exhausted and numb, but still wanting to pray. I would utter these few words: "God, please hang onto me because I have no energy to hang onto you."

That week I learned that one sentence can be enough. Prayer can be a simple, one-sentence plea.

As I traveled back and forth between my home and the home of my parents, the summer days began to unfold. We would spend several hours at a time watching my mom's favorite TV shows and snacking on gummy bears, her ultimate treat. I could begin to see the disease slowly reshaping my mom's body into a small, thin frame. Now, the thought of her not existing became a sharper point of pain.

I would finally arrive at my home on Sunday evenings depleted and depressed. I would crawl into bed and imagine myself climbing up onto God's lap as he wrapped his big-muscled, heavenly arms around me. I would lean up against him, tears dripping from my heart and feel safe, unjudged, comforted, and loved.

In those moments, I learned that pictures can be prayer. Prayer can be images in my mind.

In the months that followed, sleeping many nights in that adjacent bedroom, I would recall what a faithful companion prayer had been while I was growing up and what a limited view of it I had then. I recalled myself as a young child setting up shrines and prayer candles, trying to connect with whatever sense of God I had at that time. Now, 40 years later, in that same room, that constant companion would be called upon again and again in different ways, taking on new forms.

I learned and experienced that prayer is and can be a tool, a gateway to an extraordinary way of living. It has the power, in fact, to turn the ordinary into the extraordinary.

To me, the word *extraordinary* suggests being engaged in something uncommon. Prayer did just that. It safely opened my heart, enlarged my spirit, and expanded my thinking, creating a full, rich life even in the midst of incredible pain. It transported me to places of uncommon strength and joy.

Would you like to journey into the uncommon, the extraordinary? Incorporate the following prayer practices into your day and you'll be on your way to letting your spirit soar way beyond the challenges of your everyday life.

Prayer Practice #1: Collecting

Imagine as you go through your day that pieces of you are given away with every interaction—your relationships, your work, and the care of your home (just to name a few). I bet sometimes at the end of the day you feel that you've been pulled in many different directions, with pieces of yourself scattered all over the place. If so, it's time to collect yourself—pull yourself back together.

Taking time to collect yourself is necessary to restore your energy, gain clarity about the events of the day, and refocus on what really matters in your life. If left uncollected, you can begin to lose connection with the essence of your true self. Living as an "uncollected" self can lead to increased levels of stress, a lost sense of personal purpose, and eventually, even depression.

Did you know that your engine, the thing that keeps you running, is your heart-spirit—your soul—the essence of who you are? You give away pieces of it every day, even in a single interaction. Reclaim yourself at the end of each day with the practice of collecting.

How? Find a spot in your home where you feel safe and can be completely alone. As I explained earlier, even the bathroom can be a handy spot. Sit completely still for at least five minutes. Then take deep breaths. I recommend incorporating a formal breathing exercise regime here. Do this until you come into a state of being 100-percent present "where you are." One clue that you've attained this state is that your mind will stop racing and you will become calm.

Prayer Practice #2: Cleansing

When you think about it, cleansing or cleaning has been a part of the human culture since the beginning of time. For you, there may be a regular routine of making sure your home is in some semblance of order at the end of the day. The act of cleaning seems to add to our sense of health and well-being.

To a greater degree, cleaning as it relates to your heart-spirit should be a regular practice as well. Throughout the day, all sorts of negative elements called toxins enter your heart-spirit. They come from everywhere, as dust particles floating in the atmosphere, and they attach themselves to you, robbing you of energy, joy, and peace.

You probably have regular suppliers of toxins, perhaps a coworker, a member of your immediate family, even yourself. I'll confess, I've been my own producer of toxins, allowing critical reactions, complaining, and nagging to pollute not only my heart-spirit, but those around me as well.

At the end of each day, it may be your habit to brush your teeth or clean your face prior to climbing into bed. Why not add to that the practice of internal cleansing, making sure your heart-spirit is free of toxins that have polluted and clouded your inner beauty? Cleansing brings you back internally to a polished, shining state so that you can function at your best. It restores your state of joy and peace.

Here's a cleansing exercise you may want to practice:

Step 1: Breathe deeply, until you experience a sense of calm. (If you've done Prayer Practice #1, you're already there.)

Step 2: Begin to recall the activities of the day, focusing especially on anything that was negative or disturbing. Next, imagine a balloon. Put into the balloon any incident or feeling that you want to eliminate. Once they're all inside, imagine blowing up the balloon and letting it go, watching as it drifts into space and disappears.

Step 3: Picture yourself completely happy and at peace, engaging in your favorite and most pleasurable activities. Stay in that picture and develop as many aspects as you need until you feel 100 percent-pleasure or peace.

Now you have cleansed yourself of the day's pollutants. You are at peace and free.

Prayer Practice #3: Recollecting

Of the many prayer practices that I've encountered, recollecting has proven to be one of the most useful and effective in moving through pain and managing challenging situations. During the time my mom was dying, we spent many hours recollecting the funny and wonderful times we had together as a family.

When I want to change a negative emotional state, I start recollecting, creating a list of all the things for which I am grateful. I challenge myself to create a list of 100. Hands down, this has worked every time—by the time I get to 25 or 30, I am usually in a completely happy and peaceful mood and have captured a new sense of energy!

This wonderful, powerful practice of recollecting good things can help you gain perspective about daily experiences—good or bad. It also impacts you physiologically, releasing chemicals from your brain, causing you to feel good. Try it with your kids as well; it can very quickly turn a negative time into one that is happy and fun.

Begin by writing your list. After constant practice, all you'll need to do is start the list in your mind! Start your 100 list now.

Prayer Practice #4: Creating

Creating involves the conscious act of deciding or reminding yourself what you want your life to be. Picture yourself moving throughout your day, responding to events in a purposeful way. It's in this arena where you gain clarity about what you really want and create plans on how to make that happen.

Creating continually presents the opportunity for you to remain in control of your life, claiming determined responsibility for how you will act. This prevents us from moving into a victim mode, blaming circumstances and others when our lives do not turn out as we'd like. Instead, we can see what we can control and influence, and what action we can take.

In this prayer practice, you can also make a place and time to connect with the creative part of yourself. Creativity is an expression of your heart-spirit that allows you to constantly try and improve your current condition and develop all you were meant to be.

Are you "in tune"—"in touch"—with yourself and what your heart-spirit is saying? Do you listen to it? These prayer practices will help you do just that. Tapping into and continually nurturing this aspect of yourself will keep your heart-spirit alive, while presenting new possibilities of how to make your unique life full, satisfying, and complete.

Embrace these practices. Do them regularly. Make them the melodic habits that add a spiritual grace and rhythm to your life.

You can reach JoAnn at *www.unlockthepotential.com.*

Jill Wesley

EMBRACE DIVERSITY

The sun shone brightly above us while we played in the grass during lunch recess. I was in the 4th grade, but I can recall the scene as if it happened yesterday. I was talking, laughing, and playing with my girlfriends. It was a beautiful spring day. We were pulling dandelions from the ground, announcing our wishes for all to hear, taking deep breaths and blowing on the fuzzy flowers to make our wishes come true. Sometimes we made the dandelions twirl around by putting the stems between the palms of our hands and rubbing them together really fast. This helped the process along if the wish was particularly important or the dandelion was particularly stubborn. We watched the seeds dance in the air as they floated away on in the breeze.

Suddenly, a girl from our class came running up to us. She had a smirk on her face as she looked down at us sitting cross-legged in the grass. She took a deep breath as she prepared to deliver the big news: "Did you hear what happened at lunch today?" She looked excited and proud of herself, her eyes wide and eyebrows arched. Then she stared right at me and said, "They just voted you the ugliest girl in the whole school."

I held my dandelion tightly in my hand as I heard the "news." I looked down and immediately felt embarrassed, then deeply shamed.

I kept my eyes on my dandelion, clutched tightly in my fist, refusing to look up at her. There was an awkward silence. Her job finished, the girl marched off, presumably to spread the news.

I sat there in silence, too afraid to look up, afraid that the minute I made eye contact with anyone the tears would start streaming down my face. When I finally did look up, my friends were all busy trying to look somewhere else. No one said anything like, "That's not true!" or "You're not ugly!" Their silence hung painfully in the air around us, and I felt like I couldn't breathe, my chest tightening, my stomach sinking. When the bell rang to go back to our classrooms, they hurriedly got up and scurried away.

I sat there trying to comprehend what I had heard, trying to figure out what to do. I stared at my dandelion once again, this time through my tears. I shut my eyes as tightly as I could and made the deepest, most heartfelt wish I could make: *Please, please, please make me look like everyone else.*

The Girl In the Mirror

I walked home that day feeling defeated. I went straight to the bathroom and took a long look at myself in the mirror. It was a really painful thing to do that day. Why did I have to look the way I did? There was something wrong with almost everything on my face. My freckles were weird and embarrassing—nobody liked freckles. My lips were way too big—nobody liked big lips. My forehead was so high, we called it a "fivehead." My hair was coarse, thick, curly, and usually out of control. I couldn't dream of wearing it like my friends did. Dorothy Hamill haircut? Forget it. Farrah Fawcett hairstyle? Not a chance. Finally I looked at my skin. It was too dark.

I didn't look like anyone in my class, in my school, even in my city! My sister and I didn't even look like our parents. It wasn't fair. I was the ugliest girl in the whole school. *The whole school?* I never thought I was pretty, but I didn't know it was *that* bad. Maybe I should have seen it coming when I was cast as the lead in "Rumplestiltskin" during 2nd grade.

I stood there in silence staring at the ugly girl who looked back at me. Didn't any of my other qualities count for anything? Didn't it matter that I was smart? I did really well in school. What about being athletic? I made the softball All-Star team and earned the Presidential Physical Fitness Award. I was funny—I made the other kids laugh all the time.

Maybe my talents didn't matter. Maybe the other kids were laughing *at* me and making fun of me the whole time. I also realized that some of them seemed to feel much better about themselves once they learned that I was the "winner" of the contest. I felt so betrayed by them, but even more betrayed by the girl in the mirror.

A Tough Way to Build Character

So, by age 9, I got the message—what made me different made me ugly and inferior. My differences were something to be ashamed of.

I affectionately call the years from ages 9 to 13 my "character-building years," because there was no way I could rely on my looks to get me anything, anywhere, or anyone. Success meant doing my own thing. I decided to focus on school, sports, chorus, and drama. I wanted to fit in, but realized I couldn't, no matter how hard I tried. So I didn't try. In my mind, the universe was working against me, and, to make matters worse, it seemed to have a wicked sense of humor.

I was the only black girl in my class of 500 students. I obviously didn't have the right parents, because my mom was white and my dad was black. Every time the other kids met my mom, they would exclaim, "*That's* your mom? Are you sure? Maybe you should double check."

Then they usually asked if I was adopted.

My mom was an outspoken Democrat in a conservative town who had the nerve to make her opinions known—in her own house—even if my friends were over. She regularly talked back to the TV and voiced her disgust at reports she saw on *60 Minutes*. I had no choice but to roll my eyes, shake my head, and let out a huge sigh to let her know how much she embarrassed me.

But it didn't stop there. When I was in junior high, my parents divorced. In my mind, normal parents didn't do that. Normal parents stayed together in a miserable, unhappy marriage as some of my friends' parents did.

Did I mention that my mom is Jewish? It was always easy to find our house during the holidays—ours was the dark one, the only one without a dazzling array of beautiful, twinkling lights, without a reindeer in sight, or a jolly Santa on the roof. Sure, we got the one Hanukkah song about the dreidel at the school Christmas program, but that didn't seem to cut it. To make matters worse, I didn't wear the "right" clothes, because my mom thought it was ludicrous "to spend $30 on a pair of designer jeans that you're going to grow out of in five or six months!"

Anyone for a Second Round of Puberty?

Puberty was a tough time for most of us, a time when all of our differences were exaggerated. I'm sure many of you didn't particularly like yourselves, and all of you probably swore that your parents were put on this Earth for the sole purpose of embarrassing you in front of your friends.

I know I was different from other kids on so many levels, but I suspect many of you can relate to that feeling of not fitting in when you were growing up, even in communities where people were the same race, ethnicity, or religion. There are (and have always been) "in" groups and "out" groups and we all felt excluded at some point. We didn't have the "right" look or the "right" family or the "right" clothes. Puberty can make it feel as though everyone and everything is working against us, that nothing seems to be right, that nobody likes us or understands us.

But this feeling is not confined to our teens. Even as adults we may feel we are excluded or not good enough in our community or at work. We may hold ourselves up to unrealistic standards of beauty and success that we see in the media. We stand and look at ourselves in the mirror and pick apart our appearance. We feel that we don't fit in, that we haven't done enough with our lives, that we aren't a good enough partner, sister, daughter, or mother.

We need to stop beating ourselves up and start embracing our differences. We need to accept ourselves in order to foster an environment where our children accept their uniqueness and accept others who are different.

I'm grateful that my Mom expressed her unconditional love and support for us. She told me from a very early age that I was smart, capable, and beautiful. She told me that I wasn't a victim, that I could create my future. She told me I could do whatever I wanted to do and be whatever I wanted to be—but I had to work for it. She explained that nobody gets everything, even if they are privileged or seem to fit in. We all have to work for what we want at some point. I had to stop worrying about what other people thought and focus on being me, creating my own set of standards for beauty, success, and happiness.

Every Cocoon Eventually Opens

Luckily for all of us, things eventually change. In high school, something miraculous happened, a veritable transformation. I got my braces off, grew a few inches taller, got rid of the braids, and got my hair straightened. My face matured a bit, and I grew into my features. I could wear makeup. Suddenly, I wasn't the ugly girl anymore! My time had come.

After waiting in the wings, it was my turn to walk out into the spotlight. Suddenly there were boys, dances, cheerleading, and student government waiting for me. I wanted people to like me, and I thought it was important for them to find me attractive. I focused a lot of my energy on looking good. It may have been okay to be popular for being nice or funny, but it was much more fun to be considered attractive. I became very concerned about the way I looked, wore too much makeup, and wouldn't have dared to leave the house without it.

Now it all made sense! Maybe the key to success in life was fitting in. Fitting the mold meant that I was worthy. Fitting in meant that people would accept me.

But fitting in also meant that I had to try to hide my differences and reject who I truly was. It was exhausting staying on top of what was "in" and identifying the latest "must-have" items, styles, and looks. The problem, I soon learned, is that it is impossible to measure up— it's a never-ending pursuit. When we get caught up in trying to be perfect, or even just to be like everyone else, we miss the opportunity to develop the unique skills and talents we possess. We suffocate our authentic selves.

The Lessons I've learned

The first key to finding extraordinary success is choosing to accept yourself and being proud of who you are and where you came from. It's difficult to open up to others and accept them if you haven't accepted yourself. It is easier to focus on all of the differences and worry about fitting in, measuring up, and being judged. But your children hear the way you talk about yourself and see the way you treat yourself. Worse, they see themselves in you. If you don't accept yourself for who you are as an adult, imagine how difficult you are making it for your children!

Make a commitment to your personal growth and helping others. We don't make ourselves feel any better by insulting others just because they are different from the rest of us. As the old saying goes, "You can't build yourself up by knocking others down." Differences are to be explored, and it's okay to be curious about others. It is *not* okay to insult or attack those who are different from us.

We are all different in some way. We can teach our children that differences are to be expected in a world as big and beautiful as this one.

It took me years to become comfortable in my own skin, years spent living and traveling overseas and doing some serious soul-searching. I had to examine what my values were and find the courage to be myself. I was in my mid-20s before I not only accepted my differences, but truly embraced them and celebrated them. Today, I know my differences are a gift, something special, a source of strength. They afford me an opportunity to see the world from a very unique vantage point. My differences allow me to relate to all kinds of people. It's interesting that sometimes the things we spend years running away from are often our greatest strengths.

The second key is exploring our own biases. This will help our children grow up with fewer biases of their own. We tend to stereotype because of limited experience with other groups. Stereotyping is harmful because it ignores individual differences and encourages prejudice and discrimination. These stereotypes are often learned from our family, friends, school, and TV. Talk openly with your family—help them understand that being a member of another group doesn't automatically make others good or bad. Point out that others could stereotype your family, too!

Here's a way to make this real. Think about some of the ways Americans are stereotyped overseas: We are arrogant. We focus on making money and getting material things. We have little respect for the elderly and are afraid of getting old. We are unhappy and obsessed about the way we look, getting plastic surgery and going on diets. We live to work and we value our jobs more than spending time with people we care about. We talk so much about saving time and we create countless gadgets to save time, but we always seem to be running out of it. We are wasteful when it comes to food, water, and money.

These statements seem harsh and unfair, don't they? We often don't think about our belief system, communication style, and customs until we are confronted with something that is different from our own. We have the tendency to think that our way is the best or the only way. We rarely question our values or examine some of the stereotypes others may have of us.

Think about the language that you choose to use when you refer to groups of people who are different from you. Are you telling jokes and making fun of others? Stereotypical jokes perpetuate the myths we hold about others and dehumanize everyone involved. Do you stop and ask yourself where and how you learned this behavior? Prejudice is *learned* behavior. Do you want to teach your family to demean others? Challenge assumptions and stereotypes. Just because something is different doesn't mean it is wrong or inferior.

We are more similar than different. We all have the same core needs regardless of our racial, ethnic, or religious backgrounds, sexual orientations, marital status, physical or mental abilities. We all want the same basic things in life: a roof over our heads, food in our stomachs, and for our children to be safe.

The third key is to choose to take a few steps outside of your circle of comfort and be proactive. Be curious! Diversity is all around us. Try something new.

- ◆ Buy a world atlas and encourage your family to learn about countries heard about in school or on the news. Make learning about differences a fun project. Pick a new country each month and learn about its culture and customs, food and music.

- ◆ Look for activities that feature a culture different from your own. Eat at a restaurant, see a play, rent movies, attend festivals, visit museums, take dance classes, and listen to music.

- ◆ Select books for yourself and your family that reflect all kinds of people and ideas.

- ◆ Form a welcoming committee for new members of your neighborhood or community.

- ◆ Teach your children that another child may speak another language, have an accent, dress and behave differently, or have a different level of physical ability, but he or she wants to be asked to go out and play as much as any other child.

- ◆ Encourage your family to make friends with different kinds of people.

- ◆ Speak up when you hear someone say something that is offensive.

- ◆ Apologize if you have offended someone, even if it was unintentional. Don't judge their feelings.

The fourth key is understanding the value of diversity. According to the U.S. Census Bureau, by the year 2050, people of color will make up nearly one-half of the U.S. population. We all add value to our society and have something important to contribute. We get fresh ideas, different perspectives, and innovative solutions. We learn little from those who agree with everything we think, say, and believe. The more we expose ourselves to other cultures, the more we learn about the world. We are better equipped to work and communicate with different types of people and manage change.

Diversity is a major strength in this country. Our society is richer as a result of our differences. By valuing diversity, we can provide better client relations and customer service. Employees who work in a supportive work environment build more cohesive teams and feel better about being themselves at work.

The majority of our families came to the United States from other countries. They had to struggle to assimilate or were forced to assimilate at the cost of losing their language and customs. Centuries of tradition have faded; the meaning behind them lost within a generation or two. What a tragedy! One can certainly retain his or her own culture and be "American" at the same time.

Diversity is a reality. The United States is constantly evolving and making progress. The U.S. Constitution originally granted rights only to white, male landowners. We have made great strides since then: We've witnessed women's suffrage, the Civil Rights movement, the Feminist movement, and the end of slavery, among many others. Yet I am in my 30s, and my father went to a segregated school in the South. I am only one generation removed from institutional racism.

Ignorance breeds fear and mistrust of others. It leads to an "us versus them" mentality, to prejudice, discrimination, hate crimes, and genocide. We have the courage and strength to stand up and band together to support others. Speak up when you see injustice and discrimination around you.

Extraordinary success is about accepting yourself. It's about taking personal responsibility and about taking action. It is about having compassion, respect, and understanding for others. It is taking that first step on the journey of discovery that opens our hearts and minds. Doing so will help our children to become healthier, more empathic adults who are better prepared to live and work in our multicultural country and in the global village of the new millennium.

The more you reach out to others, the more the experience touches your heart and the more you connect with humanity. Valuing differences strengthens our world by building bridges between families, communities, and countries.

When I see dandelions now, I think of that day at school and the 9-year-old girl who felt ashamed about being different. Many things have changed, but I still make wishes. Now when I look down at my dandelion, I shut my eyes, smile, and make a wish for all of us.

Jill Wesley is dedicated to helping others reach their potential both professionally and personally. Her energetic keynotes and seminars blend stories, life experiences, and theory with her humorous, down-to-earth and inspirational speaking style. She has more than a decade of corporate and nonprofit experience working as an educator, international recruiter, and a communication trainer.

Jill has the ability to connect with any audience. She has extensive experience training thousands of people from diverse ethnic, racial, religious, and socioeconomic backgrounds. In addition to working throughout the United States and Canada, she spent six years working in Europe, Australia, Asia, and South America.

Jill currently owns her own training and consulting firm specializing in workplace communication, creativity, and humor, and valuing diversity programs. She earned a Master's in Speech and Interpersonal Communication from New York University.

Jill will make you laugh, make you think, and help you to make a difference. She may be reached at www.jillwesley.com.

Lisa Walker

HONOR THY MOTHER

"What will you name your daughter?" my nurse asked, as I lay on the hospital bed.

"Elisa," I said.

I had thought about it for months. I had thought about what it takes for an ordinary woman to have extraordinary success. I wanted my daughter's name to symbolize just that.

Elisa is my mother's—her maternal grandmother's—name. There is no more extraordinary woman I know.

"If you love you, then people will love you."

"And if you love what you represent, then people will love what you represent." Eternal words of advice from my mother, Elisa.

My mother was hurriedly dropping me off at kindergarten on "show and tell" day, although I had been loudly complaining the whole way there that I *had* nothing to show or tell. Pointing at my orange vinyl shoes, she smiled, "Use your shoes. I'm sure no one else will be wearing anything like them."

"These weird shoes?" I replied, dumbstruck. "The rest of the kids will all laugh at me.

"They'll love them if you love them," she assured me. "They'll love you if you love you."

"Don't wait for the crowd to approve of what you're doing...
...do it because it makes sense to you."

My mother has always been different, she's always known she's different, and she seems to actually *like* being different. One summer in the early 1970s, my dad purchased a movie camera so we could film the sights on our summer vacation. It took no prodding for Mom to get in front of the camera. I remember one scene in front of the White House, my mom in her black hot pants (maybe not really hot pants but definitely shorter than any shorts I would wear today at 30-plus years old), wearing a bright wig, and sashaying down the street. We kids, of course, were mortified. What would the people driving by think? Mom did not care.

One year while I was in grammar school, my brother was preparing an act for the annual talent show, lip-synching and dancing to a popular hit—"Everybody was Kung Fu Fighting." My mom was all in favor, but also wanted him to prepare a Haitian dance that I and my cousins would do with him. Now I was not ashamed of being Haitian, but Haitians represented about .09 percent of our neighborhood, so I didn't think it would exactly be a hit. Plus, my cousins I didn't even attend the school. And the traditional satin-and-white costumes, we all agreed (with the obvious exception of my mother), would make us look dumb, at best.

Needless to say, six weeks later, after far too many late-night practices with the dance instructor Mom convinced to work with us, we were getting ready to go on stage. "Remember," Mom said, "If you love you, they'll love you. If you represent Haiti with love, they'll love Haiti." We took the stage and danced energetically to the Haitian Creole music to an all-American crowd. Not only were we a hit, we actually landed several paid performances and were in all the papers!

"When you are in need of assistance don't be afraid to ask."

When Mom moved to the United States to start a new job, she left all of her family and friends behind. Even though she was working at a low-paying job, her dream was to attend cosmetology school. But she was 30-plus years old and her English was very limited. One day at work, Mom struck up a conversation with a customer named Sandy Kane. One thing led to another and before long, Sandy put Mom in contact with a friend of hers who taught cosmetology. Mom became a full-time student. When finances were tight—and they always seemed to be tight—Sandy would come through the front door like a breath of fresh air with grocery bags in tow. She was a wonderful friend to my mother, someone to whom we will always be indebted. It made me feel great when, years later, I watched Sandy's daughter, Bobbie Brown (of Bobbie Brown cosmetics), being interviewed on network television. Sandy had done so much to make my mom's dream come true, it seemed only right that her daughter had realized her own dream, too.

"No one will ever ask you to leave unless you look like you don't belong."

One night when I was 10 or so, Dad came home from work, quickly got us all cleaned up and dressed, and hurried us out the door. We were on our way to a picnic being held at Mom's place of employment. I'm not even sure I knew what she did at the time or where she worked. It was a weeknight and a 45-minute drive, but Mom had insisted that Dad bring us. When we arrived, we were tired and sleepy, but we quickly perked up as we neared the pool area. There was Mom laughing it up with the Palmolive lady from TV! Everyone was calling us over—they all wanted to meet Elisa's kids. That evening, we met Eve Arden, her husband, and members of the cast of *Sanford and Son*, all of whom were appearing at the local playhouse…where Mom worked as a masseuse! Her unique touch eventually landed her clients like Kim Zimmer, Reba McIntyre, Michelle Lee, and Dyan Cannon.

Another time, my oldest brother, Carlo, was on his way to a concert…until his date became ill. As he polished his shoes, he tried to figure out who else he could take on such short notice. Suddenly a broad smile lit up his face: "Hey Mom, are you busy tonight?"

Mom was ready and looking like a million-dollar date in 30 minutes. As Carlo made his rounds at the concert, he was asked who his knockout date was. I'm not sure if anyone really believed it was his mother!

"No one will ever ask you to leave unless you look like you don't belong."

"You have to do what you have to do."

"Success never comes easy."

My mom and my older sister Jocelyne are best friends. My mother and Jocelyne looked so much alike in their younger days that people would often mistake one for the other. Although my mother was 18 years older, it was not uncommon for her to show up at a party in matching outfits with my sister. When my sister married, my parents bought a two flat so she could stay close. A few years later, my brother-in-law had to finish his residency in another state, and my mom's best friend had to move away. My entire family accompanied them to the airport. We were all bawling our eyes out, including my dad. But I remember my mother turning to my sister—with dry eyes—and saying, "You have to do what you have to do. Success never comes easy." My mother looked at the rest of us. We got her message immediately: We needed to be strong for my sister. The tears were not helping. We all dried our eyes.

"You guys are wasting time."

My mother is always thinking forward. A phone conversation we had the other day is typical:

"I was just watching *Star Search*," she started as soon as I picked up the phone, "and a boy standing only as high as my knee won $10,000. That could have been Elisa. You're not working hard enough with her."

"Mom, she's only 5 months old."

"I know," she said. "You've already wasted five whole months."

I was laughing so hard that I "three-wayed" my sister Sindy into the conversation. When I told her what Mom had said, she started laughing, too, until Mom broke in: " Sindy, I'm sure if Jacob went on there with his guitar, he would have won, too."

"Mom, Jacob is 2 years old. And he doesn't play the guitar," Sindy said.

"That's what I mean," she responded. "You guys are wasting time."

This is the "ordinary" woman my daughter has been named after, the same woman I was named after. I don't know if I will ever overcome as many obstacles as my mother has, but she has definitely passed on all the tools that she used to achieve her success.

She taught us to give back. Mom still shops at garage sales and discount stores, not because she has to, but because it allows her to give back to the impoverished in her native country.

She taught us to treat everyone as if they held your future in their hands. Mom has welcomed both ex-cons and presidential candidates to our dinner table.

My daughter's name is Elisa, named after her grandmother.

I pray that she'll inherit so much from her grandmother:

- The courage that her grandmother showed when she was widowed at a young age and had to raise two young children by herself, until she met and married my father.
- The bravery she demonstrated when she moved to a new country in search of a better life. She lived apart from her two children and new husband for three years until she was able to bring them over.
- The willingness to take risks that her grandmother showed when starting her own company at 60-plus years old.
- The spirit of fun she demonstrates when boogying to the latest hits with her two 20-something granddaughters.
- The wisdom her grandmother often shared with her children, including the few examples I've mentioned in this brief chapter.
- The love her grandmother continues to give all of us, as when she spent four months in our home to care for her granddaughter and me after Elisa's birth.
- And finally, the vision of her grandmother, who looked at her poverty-stricken surroundings at age 12 and decided her future would be very different in her 70s. Her vision is now her reality.

Lisa's experiences range from designing and implementing U.S. aid-funded projects as a specialist for the U.S. Agency for International Development, to developing a corporate sales training program for a telecommunications company. Her diverse career set the stage for her ultimate move into speaking and training.

Her experience has made her especially effective in using creative, innovative techniques to facilitate learning while maintaining an upbeat and entertaining atmosphere. Lisa presents information in a vivid, real-world, and applicable manner. Audiences are pumped up after attending one of Lisa's programs and experiencing her fast-paced, high-energy presentations.

Debbie Metzger

SEIZE EVERY DAY

When I was a child, I thought as a child...and definitely laughed as a child. I cried like a child, and I saw things simply, like a child. I listened and spoke like a child, and I understood things like a child.

Size small was a wonderful place to be! You knew when you were in trouble, and you knew that they still loved you afterward. You knew when to flash Grandma that winning smile and how to exchange a hug for one of her amazing cookies. You knew when to put on your best manners, and no doubt learned, through some unfortunate experiences, when you could and couldn't get away with your worst.

Using crayons on actual paper got you endless praising. Your bike was your ticket to discovering the universe. You knew who your friends were. You knew what would be for dinner on Thursday. Somebody even laid out your clothes for you, and you never questioned how they magically arrived on your bed, clean and folded like that.

Life was good. Laughter came easily. You got into more trouble for having too much fun than you did for being truly naughty. Any time with your friends was reason for a party. And, on any day of the year, you knew *exactly* how many days there were until your birthday and Christmas.

That's right. We had priorities. These were the things that mattered most. We didn't ask for a lot to celebrate...just a few streamers and balloons and a couple of party games to mix the boys with the girls. Fun was the objective. Life was relatively simple.

Thinking back to those yester-times as a young girl, I am often humored, entertained, and sometimes downright inspired as I remember how the world appeared from 3 feet tall, and how every inch I grew in height brought its own new "heights" to my awareness of that world and what it had to offer.

On a good day, we could call that wisdom. With each passing year and decade, my mind saw it all in new, more complex, more "mature" and intelligent ways. A lot of what had appeared to be black and white started turning gray. Entire colors were disappearing from the palette of my life.

Consider for a moment how we defined success and happiness when we were little, and it is clear how dramatically the world has changed and how we have been changed with and by it. Today, as I look at the world through my grown-up eyes and all 67 inches of "discovery" that God granted me, you'd think I could make sense of it all after four-plus decades. But day-to-day life has a way of taking you by storm. And suddenly, you're searching for a new meaning of happiness in a grown-up world, longing to rediscover the laughter and the carefree and simple celebrations that used to be.

Then comes one of those days when God must be smiling and shaking his head, as you discover for yourself some meaningful revelation, even if in your own quirky, unique way and time. Allow me to share one of my latest.

Children are a marvelous adventure. Saying that phrase with different inflections—with or without sarcasm—can give it so many meanings, but today I truly mean it in the traditional, motherly sense of awe and delight. I have been blessed with four of those delights, of which the two youngest are my boys. They teach me the most amazing and simple things when I am wise enough (or just awake enough) to pay attention!

I remember a summer day a few years back. We were living in Minnesota. It was a particularly hectic period of my life, made more hectic as I tried to work while around the children. I appreciated and encouraged their autonomy, but still had to keep a keen eye out for suspicious activity.

One afternoon, I caught them mischievously sneaking through the kitchen with that all-too-obvious air of guilt. After a few queries and upon closer inspection, I discovered two tiny creatures hiding deep in their jeans' pockets, which in and of itself was frightening enough! After concluding that the creatures were indeed still alive and breathing after such an ordeal, we were able to identify the little fur balls as gerbils. After some discussion of the rudiments of pet care, I was eventually won over by my young son begging to keep them. Marshalling my own arsenal of negotiating weaponry against me—I distinctly remember his characterizing them as "low maintenance"—and reinforcing his arguments with a semi-toothless, melting smile, he got me to reluctantly agree to let them stay on a "trial basis."

I had no idea what a major event it was to go to the mega-super-hyper pet store. Talk about taking a trip and never leaving the farm! After a few interesting detours through some more (and less) exciting discoveries of mammal and reptile species, we finally got to the task at hand. With some help, we found everything needed for gerbil survival, including a cage complete with water bottles and food, wood shavings, and, of course, the requisite wheel for exercise. I held my ground when the boys begged for the entire playground and matching Nike outfits for the pair!

When we returned home, we quickly cleared a nice comfy area for the cage, filled it with the goods and got everyone settled. As the days passed, I kept a sharp eye on the boys' bedroom and the cage. To be fair, the kids kept their part of the bargain and did a pretty good job of caring for their new friends. I started to notice that whatever the time of day, those furry little creatures were always running around that silly wheel. It made this quiet whirring sound, which I could hear from the hall whenever I passed the room. Some days, just the sound would make me smile, as I thought of those little guys running together, like friendly neighbors on a perpetual morning jog.

Well, as life unfolds its surprises to us each day, it seems that some days are kinder than others, and likewise, so are our reactions to them. And so it was on a fateful morning not long after the gerbil invasion. Life was definitely unfolding for me, and I was not happy with its "fruits." While I was going through the motions of straightening the house, I was slowly being consumed with an attitude of the ugly sort. Walking past the boys' bedroom, I heard the familiar humming sound, and found myself placing the laundry basket down and going into their room.

The two little rodents were doing their daily cardio thing. But it didn't make me smile. Today was different. I was at war with life. It seemed like my little world was spiraling out of control. I felt myself even buying into a victim mentality, which is a cardinal sin in my life.

As I glanced at the activity in the cage, I could swear the gerbils were smiling, almost mockingly, as they jogged in cadence and rhythm to the whir of the wheel. I walked over and looked closer. Sure enough, they *were* grinning ear to ear at me, just as I thought. I bent over to get eye level with them and put my face almost against the cage. Wincing and narrowing my eyes, I said, as though accusing them of some heinous crime, "You're mocking me, aren't you?" A pause followed. And then, watching the relentless spinning and their forced motion to keep it going, I continued, "That is SO my life!" You think you're doing okay in life, and then one morning you wake up and find yourself accusing, almost threatening, innocent small animals in a cage.

I suddenly had this vision of myself, which unfolded like a scene in a bad science fiction movie, and it was not pretty. It began with my waking up to the shotgun-like sound of a morning alarm and some great hand picking me up by the scruff of the neck, dropping me into a great, steel cage, and being told, "Go on, girl, get on your wheel!" I started to run but had to keep increasing my speed to keep up. Some unseen stranger, in control of a virtual remote that controlled the speed, kept jabbing at buttons, relentlessly chiding, "Faster, faster!"

Just when I felt I was about to die from exhaustion, the big hand reached back in, picked me up, and dropped me thankfully onto my bed. "Now get some power sleep for a few hours," a deep voice intoned. "Because I'll be back to get you in the morning, and we'll do it all over again!"

Aaaaargh! I just wanted to scream! Can you appreciate the insanity? It was just so powerfully real, and so obnoxiously metaphorical.

After recovering from my initial reaction, this became a personal turning point for me. Being the eternal optimist that I am, a Mary Sunshine from birth, I surveyed the real scene of the cage, searching my mind for meaning and application and reason. I needed to make some sense of it to have mental closure.

Being a Stephen Covey fan, and believing wholeheartedly in the principle of being proactive, it suddenly occurred to me that if, indeed, I was to spend my days toiling away on the spinning wheel of my life, then by golly, I was going to have a say in it! I would choose to take a stand—to decorate my cage, to paint it wonderful colors, hang art on my wheel, bring in a stereo to play favorite music, throw some fun pillows around the floor of my cage to welcome good friends and company! Yes, I would create an environment where I could smile while I ran, where I could be surrounded by the very things that would lift my spirits and remind me personally of all that is good and inspires me to celebrate, even while I labored at my task of life. I just knew, all at once, that I had so much more control than I had previously thought, and that I was responsible for creating perspective for myself so that my happiness could prevail and find me. I was inspired and empowered.

This was the day I knew that the definition of my happiness and celebration had to change, and that no one else could define it for me, nor take it away from me once I had. It was clear the time had come to tune out the voices that would have me adapt *their* opinions, *their* judgements, *their* versions of the truth. How long had I been listening to and buying into these cries from my family, from friends, from society? Why had I allowed them to validate me (or not!), judge me, even tell me how content I should or could be?

Too long. And for no good reason. It was time to stop.

It's time for *you* to wrest control back, too. And I do mean NOW. Every day is a singular gift, a self-contained reason for rejoicing. Mark this date in red as the day you decide to choose your happiness...to take control of your mental and emotional destiny. Because every living organism is either in the process of growing or dying. Let us this day make our choice. Let us choose life!

Carpe diem, Latin for "seize the day," has now become a rallying cry in my own life. My daughter and I have matching rings with this phrase engraved as a reminder, and on occasion I find myself glancing down and catching a glimpse of those words and suddenly feeling inspired to do something I had no intention of doing moments earlier. Thankfully, I have never regretted anything that I have seized so far. And it serves as a reminder that anything I do or anywhere I go can be an adventure or a discovery when approached with a sense of exploration and childlike wonder. I'm telling you, it's learning to go back to size small—ya gotta love that inner child. She's a scream. Take her everywhere you go!

I was recently scheduled to take an early afternoon flight to conduct a business meeting the following day. As the morning became increasingly backlogged and fraught with last-minute mini-traumas, I found myself accepting the realization that I was going to miss my plane. I kept checking the car's clock on the way to the airport, somehow expecting it to care about me and prolong the minutes or cause time itself to stand still. But it didn't.

Feeling increasingly frustrated, I reminded myself that "I teach this stuff," and tried to remember the principles of flexibility and thinking outside the lines, and being positive and pro-solution instead of whining and carrying on to myself. After a few such moments of self-chiding, I circled past the airport terminal and drove right back toward the freeway ramp. I smiled as I pulled over, plugged my cell phone into the charger, filled up with gas, grabbed a soda and munchies, loaded the CD-changer with some of my favorite audios from the trunk, and jumped right back onto I-29…North.

What a great day for flying…or driving! I cued up a CD to a favorite place and started listening to one of Jack Canfield's audiobooks, feeling outrageously efficient by being able to multitask and prepare for upcoming training as I drove through the hours. With lush green valleys and fields surrounding me, and the windows down and air blowing through my hair, a soothing voice of inspiration in my ears, I thought there could not exist a more perfect "diem" to seize anywhere on this Earth. I lifted my eyes to the bluest of skies and whispered a quiet thank you, somehow feeling I had to express appreciation for this wonderful mishap that had come my way. The child rejoiced.

It is often when we least expect it that the most profound revelations come into our minds and hearts. Somehow, on this day, my mind seemed to just open up and release a flood gate of new and dazzling ideas and thoughts. Was it the breeze from the evening air or the perfect artistry of that Midwest sunset that inspired me? It was like open seating at a concert of epiphanies in my mind. I felt so energized and liberated and peaceful, all at once.

It is said that 10 percent of life is what's put on your plate and 90 percent is what you do with it. Choose to find joy in the simple things, and grace and abundance in the world we share. Choose to see with your eyes, but feel with your heart and soul. Choose to speak with your voice, but share with your very essence.

Let it be said of each of us that we lived a life of choice. Embrace that inner child, and find renewed delight and solace in her simple faith and wonder. If we succeed in doing this, we will make of life truly the perennial celebration it was intended to be.

Debbie Metzger was born and raised on the East Coast in a large family. She feels particularly blessed and inspired by the legacy of amazing women who preceded her. Her whole life has been a training ground, molding, forming, and teaching her the principles and virtues in life that she embraces and shares today. Everywhere she goes, her personal and professional goal is to "re-educate and re-inspire."

She is particularly committed to young people, and often volunteers at high schools across the country to educate students about their options and how to find opportunities that will bless their lives. She recently completed a European tour, teaching the Seven Habits of Highly Effective People (she's a huge Covey fan!) to young people in France and Belgium...*in French*.

Her ever-growing list of clients includes hospitals, pharmaceutical companies, utilities, the U.S. Navy, The Department of Transportation, the U.S. Army, Fortis Benefits, Scholastic Books, Monster.com, and her personal favorite, Harley-Davidson, because it reminds her that "what doesn't kill ya, makes ya stronger!"

Claudia A. James

LET YOUR LIGHT SHINE

On this cold winter afternoon, a slight chill penetrates my body as I sit at my kitchen table. Gazing through the kitchen window, I watch winter lay a fresh blanket of snow on my veranda. My black wrought iron furniture is now covered with another layer of nature's purity. The plump orange-breasted robin, once perched on the bird feeder, has gone elsewhere for food. There are no sounds in the house other than my fingers tapping on the computer keyboard, the humming of the refrigerator's motor, and the ticking of the mantel clock.

My once-tidy kitchen has been turned into a convalescent area—the kitchen chairs have been moved against the walls to make room for my wheelchair, and a walker stands in one corner of the room. The louver doors leading to the dining room have been removed; so have the ones leading to the living room. My bed is now stationed in one corner of the living room.

The phone rings. It's one of my close friends wintering in Florida. When I tell her what has happened and how my spirit is wounded, she responds, "No, Claudia, not you—your light always shines."

Ten days ago, I fell down a full flight of stairs in my home. Just yesterday I had the courage to look at the staircase and count the stairs—there are 14. My accident happened in the early morning hours when I was making my way from my bedroom on the second floor to the kitchen on the first floor for morning's first eye-opening experience: coffee. As I began falling, I heard the bones breaking in my left ankle and I watched my foot flop from one step to another. When I finally landed on the tile floor at the bottom of the steps, my foot was in an unnatural position, and the pain was excruciating.

I distinctly remember thinking, perhaps even saying, *No, I can't go through this again!* The previous 18 months had been a series of non-stop surgeries, doctor's visits, hospital visits, medications, hospital bills, and lost work. I thought this year would be easier!

I had no sooner uttered those words when I heard a stern voice—clearly from my late mother, who loathed self-pity: "Very few people die from a broken ankle. So get on with your life!" I laid my face on the foyer's cold tile floor to avoid passing out and began developing a strategy for getting help—unlocking the front door so the paramedics could get in and getting to a phone so I could call them. Because I was so close to the front door, I decided to unlock it first. Dragging my body to the door, I reached up to twist the deadbolt and open the door slightly. At that moment, I heard a most unwelcome noise—the *beep-beep-beep* of my security alarm. Six more beeps and the alarm would go off.

Emotionally I knew I couldn't tolerate the ear-iercing shrill of the alarm, the resulting unanswerable phone calls, and the pain I was experiencing. My strategy now included an extra step—getting to the alarm's keypad before the alarm went off. Once I deactivated the alarm, I headed to the kitchen phone. Having dragged my body for what seemed like an eternity, I collapsed by the phone and put the right side of my face on the cold kitchen floor to avoid passing out again. Tears were now streaming down my face as I no longer denied the pain. After gaining my composure, I decided to call my adult daughter rather than 911, so I would not encounter an ambulance bill.

My daughter and a neighbor helped me into my car and drove me to the hospital. Six hours later, I was having a steel plate put in my ankle. Twenty-eight hours later, I returned home with a wounded spirit,

facing more hospital visits, doctor visits, medical bills, speaking can-
cellations, and lost income. I thought my light had gone out for sure.

Letting our light shine is not something we consciously do. It is,
rather, a spontaneous illumination that occurs automatically, whether
we're experiencing good times or bad. This spontaneity is the result of
continually taking detours as we drive down life's road. These detours
require that we break from tradition, that we embrace our individuality.

Detour #1: Keeping a Positive Attitude

When you hear the familiar lyrics, "This little light of mine, I'm
gonna let it shine," do you inwardly say, "Yes, I am"? But then things
happen and, before you know it, you've volunteered to chair the negativity committee.

That won't happen if you routinely fill your mind with positive
thoughts. To accomplish this, surround yourself with positive people,
take in only positive information, and *begin* as well as *end* each day
with positive thoughts.

A 21-day plan for developing a positive attitude

- Begin each day by getting up when the alarm first goes off—don't
  hit the snooze button; that's indirectly saying no to life.

- Include a 15-minute devotional time in your morning's routine.
  Focus on a specific word, quote, or scripture. If other thoughts
  come into your mind, don't fight them, just let them come and go.
  Let the devotional subject be your guide for the day. End your
  devotional time by remembering the words of the great prophet
  Kahlil Gibran: "Awake at dawn with a winged heart and give thanks
  for another day of loving."

- Memorize part or all of a new poem and/or scripture each day—
  recite it when negative thoughts enter your mind during the day.

- Throughout the day, write your negative thoughts on a piece of
  paper. Before you go to bed, rewrite every negative thought in
  positive language on another piece of paper. Then crumble up the
  paper filled with your negative thoughts and throw it away.

◆ Finish your day by listing all the positive—not the negative—things
that happened during the day. And, as you drift off to sleep, repeat
the word "Yes!" This will help you end the day with a relaxing
smile and will set the stage that your subconscious mind will fill
with positive thoughts as you slumber.

Detour #2: Discovering Yourself

In his book *The Seven Habits of Highly Effective People,* Stephen Covey
wrote that most people "live life by default." In other words, they live
in a reactive state, letting the events of life direct their path, rather
than living in a proactive state, letting their internal light direct their
path.

To begin this detour of self-discovery, I recommend you complete
the following formal and informal assessments: the Strong-Campbell
Interest Inventory, the Myers-Briggs Type Indicator (MBTI), the Cali-
fornia Personality Profile, and a values clarification. The first three
assessments need to be administered by a professional, such as a career counselor or psychologist, who can help you evaluate the results.
The fourth is one you can do on your own—simply create a list of the
things that are important to you, such as a family, honesty, education,
etc. This assessment is a key tool in understanding where some of
your stress is coming from—it often comes from living out someone
else's values.

After you spend time in reflection and complete all of these assessments, you will be equipped to create a one- or two-paragraph
description of who you are and what you are about: your personal
mission statement.

Taking this detour will keep you from driving on the wrong side of
Life's road.

Detour #3: Respecting Your Uniqueness

Through your detour of self-discovery, you learned some new things about yourself, and perhaps affirmed some things you already knew, the most important of which is that you are a unique person. To let your light shine even brighter, you must respect your uniqueness so others can see the authentic you.

Practical steps

- Untie the ropes that bind you to others; let go of needing their approval.
- Nurture your inner child; take time to play.
- Learn something new every day, perhaps a new word.
- Quantify your gifts; articulate your strengths.
- Unify your body, mind, and spirit; balance your daily life between all three.
- Express your thoughts, feelings, and opinions by using the pronoun *I*—use it more than the pronoun *you*.
- Approach others openly, honestly, and directly. NICE is a four-letter word you do not want used to describe you.
- Stake your claim. Articulate your accomplishments; review the things you crossed off your "to-do" lists yesterday.
- Strive for excellence, not perfection.
- Remember: *You* are someone's role model.

Detour #4: Embracing Change

Change is the only constant aspect of life, so embrace it and accept the challenge of being stretched beyond your comfort zone when change occurs. Realize that life is an evolution requiring us to learn new things and apply those new things. As you find yourself stretching and making mistakes, remember the words of my late father: "If you're not making one mistake a day, you're not doing enough."

To move comfortably through change:

- ◆ Affirm your negative feelings, but don't get stuck in negative thought.
- ◆ Determine what you can and cannot control.
- ◆ Ask for help from someone who will listen to you but not commiserate with you.
- ◆ Breath deeply, recalling these powerful words spoken by an old, country minister: "Out of chaos will come order, are ya listenin'?"

Detour #5: Listening to Your Intuition

Are ya listenin' to your gut? Your intuitive messages are calling you to action, so avoid second-guessing them. To affirm their validity, keep a log of your "callings" for the next month, whether you act on them or not. At the end of the month, review your log—how many times did you need to take action and didn't?

Detour #6: Leaving a Legacy

The legacy you leave will impact generations to come. To make certain you're leaving the legacy you want, write your epitaph now, then ask your friends and family members if they concur with what you have written. If they don't, ask them to write your epitaph based on their perceptions of your behavior so far.

If you decide theirs is better than yours, you may want to just keep doing what you've been doing. On the other hand, you may decide that you need to make some behavioral changes to change their perceptions of you and create the legacy you are proud of.

Winter has acquiesced her shielding skies to Spring's bright sun, and her blankets of snow to Spring's brushstrokes of color. I now sit on the veranda, in the chairs once covered by snow, and gaze into the kitchen window remembering the hours I spent longing for Spring's renewal.

The wheelchair has been put away, the bed removed, and the louver doors replaced.

The cast is gone, only crutches remain.

And each day I give thanks for this recent detour; life's road is now a little smoother.

My good friend has returned from Florida. She, like others, tells me my light is shining brighter than ever.

Claudia may be reached via e-mail at jemscaj@aol.com or by phone: 816-420-8686.